To Kyle

The Prisoners and the Paintings

Reading rocks !!

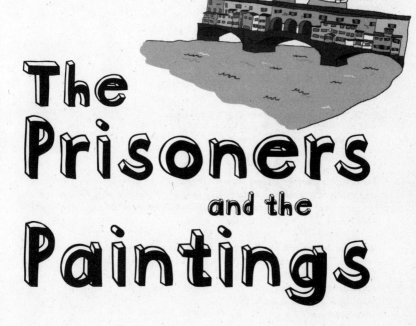

The
Prisoners
and the
Paintings

David A. Poulsen

KEY PORTER BOOKS

Library and Archives Canada Cataloguing in Publication

Poulsen, David A., 1946-
    The prisoners and the paintings / David A. Poulsen.

(Salt & Pepper chronicles ; #5)

ISBN 978-1-55470-015-8

I. Title. II. Series: Poulsen, David A., 1946- . Salt & Pepper.
chronicles ; 5

PS8581.O848P75 2008   jC813'.54   C2007-906677-1

 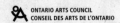

The publisher gratefully acknowledges the support of the Canada Council for the Arts and the Ontario Arts Council for its publishing program. We acknowledge the support of the Government of Ontario through the Ontario Media Development Corporation's Ontario Book Initiative.

We acknowledge the financial support of the Government of Canada through the Book Publishing Industry Development Program (BPIDP) for our publishing activities.

Key Porter Books Limited
Six Adelaide Street East, Tenth Floor
Toronto, Ontario
Canada M5C 1H6

www.keyporter.com

Electronic formatting: Alison Carr

Printed and bound in Canada

08 09 10 11 12 6 5 4 3 2 1

*For Linda, my wonderful editor,
who makes what I do so much better. In fact,
she's so good that I forgive her for
not being a Yankees fan!*

1

My Brother, the Artist?

My brother was grinning at me as I came through the front door. That's never a good thing. But the even weirder part was that my parents were looking at me pretty much the same way. Grinning, I mean. And it was creeping me out.

Okay, the first thing you have to understand is that my brother was put on this planet to fill my life with moments that are just about as pleasant as, say, having a root canal. Or getting a tetanus shot. Or swallowing a fly. Believe me, I know this because all of those things have happened to me and all of them are zero fun. And the *most* zero fun thing of all is having Hal Elway Bellamy for a little brother.

Some of my worst little-brother-horrors have started with him grinning at me. About like he was at that exact moment. So you can understand why I walked into the living room at about the same speed a bomb disposal guy approaches an abandoned backpack in a mall.

As I did I looked a little more closely at Mom and Dad. Yep, no doubt about it—they were also doing the Cheshire cat thing. And my best friend Pepper was sitting in the big, sort of purple-brown easy chair that I love to sit in when I'm reading. Except Pepper wasn't reading. You guessed it—she was grinning. At me.

That meant that the only person who wasn't grinning at me was my older sister Janet. There were two reasons for that. One, Janet was too grouchy to grin. The odd smirk maybe and a snarl now and then. But not many grins. Oh, and Janet was also off at Colorado State University. She was majoring in grouchy.

I thought about going back outside and coming in again. It was like everyone I knew had been popping stupid pills while I'd been at our outdoor arena practising barrel racing on my quarter horse gelding, Bugsy. We were getting ready for a high school rodeo that was happening the next Saturday and I'd been riding every day after school.

But on this day while I'd been out riding, obviously somebody had slipped something into the soda floats I noticed everyone was drinking. Everyone except me.

So there I was with no float and no grin on my face. Talk about feeling totally out of place.

"Anybody want to tell me what this is about?"

"Good news, Christine," my mom said.

"Judging from the look on everyone's face and the fact that Pepper is here, I'm thinking we must have won the lottery."

The weird thing is that even as I was saying it—all sarcastic, like there was no way *that* was what everybody was totally happy about—there was a little part of me that was thinking, "what if that *was* it?"

I mean, what would it be like to be going along and, whoops, there's ten million dollars that you have today that you didn't have yesterday? What would someone do with all that money? Someone like, say, me? I didn't have an answer to the question. I mean, other than paying some kidnappers to deposit my brother in some country nobody had ever heard of—like Littlecreepistan—I had no idea what I'd do if we were suddenly rich.

But that wasn't it. My brother was holding up a painting, a pretty good one. I thought I recognized it—it was something he'd done a while back for school or some contest. I remembered him showing it to me, but to be honest I hadn't been paying real close attention. Like I said, it was an okay painting, one of his better ones actually, because it was of a horse race. Not a barrel horse race but a horse race with a bunch of horses on a track. And there were buildings in the background ... houses and one real big building like a castle or something.

I never thought of my brother's art as any big deal. He'd been drawing and painting for as long as I can remember. But, to be honest, I put Hal's art in the same category as his baseball cards and his superhero comic book collection. It was just stuff that my brother had. And if I was in a really good mood I might even let him take all of it to Littlecreepistan.

"Not the lottery but we won . . . actually *I* won," my brother said. It wasn't even the loud, tinny voice he uses whenever the Blue Jays are playing and he yells, "We won!" just to annoy me.

He just said it and then set the painting down so it was leaning against the couch. This time I looked at it more closely. Actually I stared at it. That was the weird part. It was like the painting *wanted* me to look at it more closely. To stare at it. Like it was telling me to do that.

One of the horses was in the foreground. Its muscles were rippling and there were beads of sweat here and there on the brown body. Its mane was flying back and every part of its body was working, straining to give out maximum effort.

I've always wondered if Bugsy actually cared about winning or if it was just instinct and wanting to please me that made him try really hard every time we ran the barrels. In Hal's painting you just knew that the horse wanted to win. All the horses did. And somehow Hal had captured that feeling. Especially with the horse in the foreground. It was like I could feel its power, almost hear its hooves pounding the ground. And behind it, more horses, each rider wearing different colours, every face grimacing from the effort of controlling the powerful mounts as they careened around the course.

I realized that I'd been wrong before. This wasn't just okay, or even pretty good. The painting was amazing. Amazing as in, *my brother had talent.*

DAVID A. POULSEN ‡ 11

"The race," I said. "Where is it?"

"It's called the Palio," Hal explained. "It happens every year in a place called Siena. That's in Italy. They race right through the streets of the city."

"Okay, I have to admit, it's really good. But why did you choose that race to paint? Why not choose one that was closer to home?"

Hal looked at me funny. "That's the weird thing," he said slowly. "I don't know. It was like something was telling me this is what I should paint. So I went on my computer and Googled the Palio and—"

"Whoa!" I interrupted. "Something was *telling* you? What does that mean?"

Of course, I knew exactly what he was talking about. After all, the painting had just done the same thing to me.

"I don't know exactly." Hal shook his head slowly. "I just knew that I had to paint that scene. I could see it in my head and everything."

"Cool," Pepper breathed.

I knew what she was thinking . . . a mystery. I decided to change the subject in a hurry.

"So what did you win?" I figured it would be some okay prize like sneakers or a hoodie or a month of free slurpees.

"It's huge," my brother grinned and I could see my parents' heads bobbing up and down behind him.

Okay, so maybe three months of free slurpees. That would get us through summer—not bad.

"Thanks to me, you've got yourself a free trip. Because

I get to take my family along so they can see my painting hanging right there in the middle of all that greatness."

A *trip*, I thought to myself. It can't be to anywhere, like, *really* excellent. I mean, this *was* my brother so I was thinking Winnipeg or maybe Cleveland, something like that.

"So where's this big trip taking us?" I asked. I was kind of hoping for Cleveland. I'd always wanted to check out the Rock and Roll Hall of Fame. Besides, Winnipeg is in Manitoba and all it's famous for is cold in the winter and mosquitoes in the summer.

I was wrong. Totally wrong.

"Florence—that's in Italy, too—to one of the most important art galleries in the world. Am I cool or am I cool?"

"First of all," I glared at my brother, "I know where Florence is. Second of all ... "

I realized there was no second of all so I sat down. On the couch, since my favourite chair was still occupied.

"It's true, Christine." My dad was nodding now, nodding *and* grinning. "Hal submitted the painting to an international competition and he's one of ten kids from around the world who will have their paintings hanging in the Uffizi Gallery in Florence for a whole month."

"Yeah, so I guess you two aren't the only ones who can win a contest." Hal picked up the painting and displayed it all over again. Of course he was talking about the competition Pepper and I had won the year before. We'd submitted an essay to the National Archaeologists Association contest and it won us a trip to a dig in New Mexico. As usual, things had gotten a little crazy after that. You might remember—I wrote about it in *No Time Like the Past*.

I had to admit this was a pretty big deal. An international art competition and a gallery in Florence, Italy. The bad part was we'd never hear the end of it from Hal. The good part was we were going to Italy. The whole family. But that didn't explain why Pepper was grinning. Last time I checked she wasn't part of our family.

She must have read my mind. "And I'm going, too. My mom and dad were already planning a trip to Europe so I get to go with you guys and then they're going to come over later and I can meet them for our vacation."

At last, some good news. No, that wasn't true. It was actually pretty great that my brother had won the contest and it was even better that we were going to Italy. But Pepper coming, too? Now that was sweet.

"But if you won a contest in Italy, how ... what's the painting doing here in our house? Shouldn't it be over there somewhere?" (I waved in what I hoped was the direction of Italy.)

"Actually we scanned it and sent it by e-mail for the contest. That's what all the artists who entered the competition did. Mom helped me."

"We scanned it at the university's computer lab," Mom said. That made sense. Mom had gone back to university a couple of years before.

"And not only did your brother's talent result in his work being displayed next to the greatest art works in the world," Dad beamed, "your mom and I will finally have a chance to do something we've been wanting to do for a very long time. The best man at our wedding was Mel Blitzer. He and his wife Ellie have been living in Florence for fifteen years and we keep saying we're going to visit them. Thanks to Hal," another big smile in Hal's direc- tion—*gag me*, "we'll finally be able to do that."

Okay, I had to admit that it was all very nice. But there was one thing that was keeping me from going all crazy with cele- brating. Whenever Pepper and I went anywhere together, whether it was to England or New Mexico or Alaska, it seemed we found ourselves caught up in the middle of some mystery. And with those mysteries came vicious vampires, zonked-out zombies and brawling bad guys from a thousand years ago. Not exactly the sort of people someone like me— who likes nothing better than a good book and a cup of hot chocolate—needs to spend a whole lot of time with.

I promised myself right then and there that this would be a trip with no mystery, no chasing after bad guys, no breakneck excitement and definitely nothing that could ever be called a Salt and Pepper Chronicle.

I just wanted a quiet trip to Italy, with lots of Italian food, lots of sun tanning, lots of getting around to the tourist spots and maybe even a chance meeting with a cute Italian boy—that sort of thing.

I probably should have guessed my life wasn't about to go the way I planned. It never had before, so why would it start now?

2

The Mystery Man

I certainly should have suspected something later that night. I couldn't sleep. I kept thinking about Hal's painting—the one of the horses in that race. I couldn't get it out of my mind. Not only was it really good, it was almost spooky good—whatever that means. I finally decided to get out of bed, tiptoe down to the living room and look at it again. Maybe then I'd actually be able to get some sleep.

Everyone in the house was sleeping except Buck, the dog we had adopted (or maybe he adopted us) after our last major adventure in Alaska. Buck was a Husky and not much fazed him, so he lay there on his mat looking at me, a little curious but that's it. Buck wasn't the kind of dog that would suddenly start barking like he'd lost his dog mind. Unless, of course, the person prowling around our living room at night wasn't a member of our family. Then he'd swing into action and Buck in action was a pretty amazing thing as we had found out in Anchorage. (I wrote about *that* in *The Book of Vampire*.)

I turned on a lamp so I could see the painting a little better. I stared at it for a long time. And I have to be honest; I was pretty much knocked out by my brother's artistic ability. But there was something else—I know this part sounds weird but the longer I looked at the painting, the more I felt, I don't know, strange. It was . . . it was like the painting was trying to say something to me. I don't mean like in *Harry Potter* where the figures in the paintings talk, but it was as if there was some message . . . something that I was supposed to know.

I decided to look at each part of the painting by itself to see if whatever I was supposed to know would suddenly be clear to me. First I looked at the upper left corner. That was mostly sky and buildings, rooftops, and the castle, if that's what it was, further in the background. But I didn't have "the feeling," whatever that feeling was, when I looked at that part of the painting.

Upper right was next. It showed a couple of the horses that were further back in the race. There was a wall behind them and some spectators, too. But they were far away so you couldn't make out their faces.

Next I concentrated on the lower left corner of the picture. More horses, some houses behind them. I loved that part. The horses and their riders—Hal had done an amazing job of making them real. Then, finally, the lower right, with the brown horse in the lead. Part of his body was on the left side of the picture but most of him was on the right. I focused on him for a long time, and just like before it was almost as if I could hear him running and feel his strength as he hurtled down the street just ahead of the rest. I stared at that part for a while.

And that's when I saw it. Just above the horse, standing in a sort of balcony thing on one of the houses that lined the route, was a man—an old man. He was different from the spectators, who were in the background and kind of hazy. Hal had painted this guy in detail so I could see everything about him—the lines that creased his weathered old face, the red shirt that hung open like it was too hot to button it up and a brown cloth cap that looked almost as old as the man himself.

But something felt wrong ... out of place, like my brother had made a mistake. The man wasn't watching the race. He wasn't looking at the horses going by right below him.

He was looking at me!

And he was pointing. It was hard to tell what he was pointing at, but the more I looked, the more it seemed like he was pointing up the street—in the direction the horses had come from. I know it sounds weird—totally weird—but it really felt like he was trying to tell me something; that maybe there was something back there I should be looking at. Or looking *for*. The problem was that the painting didn't go that far. It stopped before there was anything on the street to see except for the race.

I shook my head and I actually rubbed my eyes, you know, like you see characters do in cartoons. And I looked at the painting again. Nothing had changed—the old man was still standing on the balcony looking right at me and pointing.

———•◦•———

"Psst, Hal."

"Hnnh, go 'way."

My brother shifted in bed and rolled over.

"Hal, wake up." I shook him.

He didn't move and this time he didn't even moan. He just went back to the sleep-breathing of an eleven-year-old twerp.

I shook harder. This time he turned his head, opened one eye and looked up at me. He didn't look happy.

"The house better be on fire," he growled, "because if you interrupted my dream about me and those two amazing supermodels water-skiing together for anything less than a major blaze, I'm going to figure out a way to turn your nose into a zucchini and people will come from all over the world to see—"

"Get up." I hissed at him. "Now."

Hal made like he was going to roll back over and pull the covers over his head.

"If you're not out of that bed in five seconds I'm going for cold water." I figured that threat would get him moving because he knew that I'd do it. Mostly because I'd done it before.

"I can't."

"What do you mean you can't?"

"I'm naked."

"Eww!"

I couldn't think of anything in the world more gross than my brother's naked self getting out from under the covers. And even though I knew he was probably lying I couldn't take the chance.

"Okay, I'll wait outside the door," I told him. "I'll give you thirty seconds to get dressed and get out there."

I stepped outside and closed the door gently. Then I thought of something. Something that would get him moving for sure. I pressed my face to the door. "Something's happened to your painting," I whispered loudly.

He was out the door in maybe ten seconds . . . wearing pajama bottoms. No shirt, which was bad enough, but if he'd had nothing on the bottom half—double eww!

"What—what's wrong with my painting? Where is it? Has it been stolen? Omigod, they've stolen my painting. That happens sometimes with masterpieces. I just knew—"

"The painting is right where it was—in the living room, but there's something I have to ask you about it."

"You woke me up for that?"

"Yeah, come on."

I led him into the living room. I could hear his bare feet slapping the floor behind me, louder than necessary. My brother's irritating and childish little protest.

I knelt down in front of the painting and Hal knelt

down beside me. "The guy on the balcony—the one who's pointing—was he part of, you know, what you said about something telling you what you should paint?" I looked hard at Hal to see if he was getting what I was asking him.

He looked back at me. "What guy on the balcony?"

I turned and pointed at the part of the painting that had grabbed me earlier. "That guy right th—" I stopped in mid-sentence and stared at the balcony. There was no one there. No old man. No one. I bent down close so my face was almost right against the canvas.

There was no one on that balcony.

"What are you talking about?" Hal was doing his "my sister is an idiot" voice and, to be honest, right at that moment I felt like one. I turned back to Hal.

"Hal, this is really important. When you painted this picture . . . was there a man on the balcony on that house—that one right there?" I pointed again at the painting.

"I always knew you needed major counselling, but this is the worst yet," he was shaking his head. "You can see the painting. You can see the balcony. There is no old man. There has never been an old man." He pronounced every syllable slowly and distinctly to emphasize how dumb I was.

"And now I'm going back to bed where I hope my supermodel friends and I will continue having what was a very nice time until you came along."

He stomped off, his bare feet even louder than before.

I couldn't really blame him. I stared at the painting for at least five more minutes and nothing changed. Finally, I gave up and wandered off in the direction of my bedroom. I knew that, unlike my brother, I would not be having a terrific dream. In fact, I doubted I'd be getting a whole lot of sleep that night.

I did make one major decision, though. I decided right then and there not to tell Pepper about the man in the picture. This was one trip that wasn't going to end up with all of us caught up in some mystery. And if I even hinted to Pepper about a guy who points and disappears, she'd be all over that like ugly on my brother. (Actually, when my dad says it, it's "ugly on an ape," but I like my version better.)

3

I'll Show You Talent

I was right. I tossed and turned, got up three times for water, two other times to go to the bathroom (thanks to the water), read my book for a while and even took deep breaths and counted sheep. Nothing worked. It was a lost night. The one thing I didn't do was go back and look at the painting again. I'd had about enough of weird paintings for one night. Actually for a lifetime.

And in the back of my mind was this nagging thought that the trip to Italy might just turn out to be as stressful and scary as all the other trips we'd been on over the last few years.

I know what you're thinking. What kind of grade nine (almost) graduate lets herself get caught up in all the stuff that's happened to me? The answer is . . . I don't know. I mean, I can't understand how a totally normal person keeps getting into near-death experiences that would scare the bejeebers out of James Bond, Spiderman and maybe even all those CSI types.

Actually, I blame my brother (you already know about him) and my best friend. Let me tell you about her. Pepper McKenzie's two main reasons for getting up in the morning are:

1. There might be an adventure just waiting to happen;
2. There might be a totally amazing boy just dying to meet her.

I'm not totally opposed to the second point on her list, but that whole adventure thing is extremely overrated.

Pepper, with her red hair, freckles, cute face and the beginnings of an actual figure (I'm still waiting for *that* to happen), has been my best friend since her family moved to Riverbend when we were both mere children. And for a long time, things were fine. We agreed on most stuff— what music to listen to, what movies to rent, what guys in what groups were the cutest (I'm all about Coldplay and Pepper is major into Fall Out Boy), what to do to my brother if he bugged us *one more time*—all the important things.

But then everything started to change. Ever since we went off to England on what was supposed to be a pleasant summer vacation, it's all been different. That was when we met Simon Chelling and the vampires and instead of a quiet restful holiday, we ended up in the middle of this vampire gang war.

That was not a lot of laughs.

At least not for me. Pepper and Hal seemed to love it. The more dangerous things got, the better they liked it. And the worst part? Now it seems like every time I turn around I get thrown into some new mystery with scary stuff happening all around me. It's like my life isn't mine anymore. I'm this teen detective who doesn't want to be one. (Well, okay, I have to admit I get to go to some cool places and some of the adventures are *sort of* fun. But so is a hot bath and a good book, you know what I mean?)

The last week of school flew by. I got through the day after my no-sleep night, mostly because it was a study and review day. For me, it turned into seven hours of trying to keep my head from falling forward and going *clunk* on my desk. The rest of the week was tough. I had two final exams on the same day—English and math—this totally long and boring assignment to finish for French, my locker to clean out (that took most of Wednesday) *and* I had to race home after school every night so I could practise on Bugsy.

So I didn't have time to pay attention to Hal. I did notice that he was running around trying to organize everybody like he was Mom or something. Which was completely ridiculous because my brother is the most disorganized person on the planet. The last forty-five seconds or so before we have to run out of the house to the school bus every morning are like something off *America's Funniest Home Videos*. Hal is usually trying to brush his teeth, find a missing sock, get his books into his backpack and check his lunch to make sure Mom didn't sneak something healthy in there. Oh yeah, and he has to admire himself in the mirror a couple of times on the way to the front door.

So you can understand why no one was really into my brother's sudden interest in organizing the world. As for me, I don't think it had completely registered that we were going to Italy in less than three weeks.

Even though I'd sworn that I'd never look at Hal's painting again, I found myself sneaking down to the living room a couple of times to check it out. The old man on the balcony never reappeared and I was pretty close to convincing myself I had imagined the whole thing. Pretty close, but not quite.

There was something else, too. I hate to admit it but I think I was a little jealous. Here was my brother—who I'd always figured was the biggest loser since Napoleon (didn't he lose a bunch of wars and stuff?)—turning out to be this amazing artist with his painting going off to hang in an art gallery in Italy—not Winnipeg or Cleveland. *Italy*.

I realized that except for one essay—one lousy essay that got us to an archaeological dig outside Albuquerque, New Mexico—I'd done exactly nothing that was really good in my whole life. And let's face it. Albuquerque isn't exactly Florence, Italy.

To make myself feel better I decided I'd sit down and write a poem. Some people said I was pretty good at poetry. Well, okay, maybe it was only Mom and Dad who said that, but I remember my fourth grade teacher telling me that my Christmas haiku was . . . uh . . . very original. Or something like that.

So, a poem it was to be. I'd show the world that my brother wasn't the only Bellamy with creative talent. First, I had to think of something to write about. I didn't have a boyfriend, so I couldn't write one of those really bad poems about how he didn't love me and the world was, like, totally black and horrible. And Buck hadn't died so I couldn't really write a tragic favourite-animal-death poem. I had noticed that we seemed to be short a couple of goldfish lately, but how tragic can a missing-goldfish-poem be?

I decided to take the advice of this author who had come to our school the year before. He said you should write about stuff that you know. I decided to write about cleaning out my locker. I knew that subject *very* well. The poem went like this:

Locker Day at School

A sandwich, all black, it was ham once, I think,
And gum without wrappers, that used to be pink.
A book but no cover, I don't know its name
Two chocolate milk cartons, empty, a shame.
A note from Greg Mullins that tells how he hates me
On a one to ten scale, it's a two that he rates me.
A shoe with no laces, it's left, where's the right?
A hoodie too small and way, way too tight.

A pencil, two pens and seven red crayons
A puzzle, and part of a Gameboy to play on.
A knife, a bent fork and a very nice spoon
My mom wasn't pleased when I lost them last June.
A notebook for Social, I sure could have used it
That test was a killer—I should have refused it.
And right near the bottom my favourite socks
And smelling like each had been worn by ten jocks.
A Coldplay CD and three bags of chips
All crushed and all bent—shaped like small paper clips.
In the whole rotten place there's not much about school
But Pepper keeps saying gross lockers are cool.
Still I guess I can't blame my teacher Miss Walker
For yelling my name—"Yo, Christine, clean that locker!"

Okay maybe it'll never be displayed on a wall in some famous castle in Europe, but I felt better after I'd written it.

That's my name, by the way…Christine Louise Bellamy. Although I'm actually getting used to "Salt." I get that because my best friend is "Pepper." Great. I'm one half of a set of condiments. And every time we solve another mystery, more people call me Salt. That's another thing I hate about the whole mystery-adventure thing. But, not much I can do about that. Not yet anyway. If I ever have one of my poems published, though, I think I'll use one of those fake names like some writers do. I won't be Salt or even Christine Bellamy. It'll be some totally amazing name that tells the world that the person with this name is talented, beautiful, sexy, smart and some day will have an actual figure.

And that was my last thought as I fell asleep the night before the rodeo. What name would I use? Tarla Winchester . . . Bobby-Rose Rivers . . . Royal Blue . . . Blue Royal . . . Cincinnati de la Cruz . . . Linda. . . .

The rodeo was totally fun. And Bugsy was awesome. In case you don't know about barrel racing, it's a cloverleaf pattern around three barrels and a run back to the start/finish line. If you knock down a barrel you get a five-second penalty.

Because it was the finals for the year, everybody had to make two runs and the fastest on the two runs would be the winner. Bugsy and I made our two best runs of the year and ended up in second place. And even though I would have liked to win, the cool part was that the top two people in all the events would be going to Calgary, Alberta, later in the summer to represent our district against all the other districts in the United States and Canada.

Which meant this would be, like, my busiest summer ever. First Italy and then Calgary. Excellent!

Oh yeah, Italy. I wasn't sure how excellent that part was going to be. I mean, Florence and all that and a trip with my family and Pepper—yeah, that part would be great. But then there was the fact that my brother would be there, too. And not only would he be there but he'd be, like, the star of the trip. And Hal can be pretty disgusting even when he's *not* the centre of attention.

Hey Buddy, Wanna Buy a Watch?

It didn't take long for Hal to prove my point. The guy just wasn't going to handle success and fame well.

We were shopping on the Ponte Vecchio, which is this amazing bridge in Florence. Serious, there are shops, especially jewellery shops, on this bridge. The bridge is six hundred years old and it spans the River Arno in Florence. It was mid-morning and already the hot Italian sun was turning the city into an outdoor sauna.

The flight the day before had been fine except for Hal trying to impress the female flight attendant. He was doing his adult number. He ordered a scotch and Dr. Pepper! She brought him a Dr. Pepper. Then Hal asked her if he could dial up an adult movie called *Women in Bondage*. The attendant told Hal he was barely James Bond–age. I totally liked that flight attendant.

Our hotel in Florence was, like, fancy-schmancy and

Pepper and I had our own room. Hal was with Mom and Dad. We had eaten breakfast on this terrace looking out over the city and I have to admit it was pretty awesome. Maybe Italy was going to be an okay (and normal) vacation after all. The reception to honour the contest-winning artists whose paintings would hang in the Uffizi for the next month was scheduled for later that day, which left ample time for shopping. I like shopping, but Pepper is *in love* with the whole concept and was enjoying herself, to say the least. We'd already hit some of the leather shops (Florence is famous for leather jackets, purses and everything else leather), and Pepper had bought a very cool purse earlier that morning in the Piazza di San Giovanni.

Anyway, there we were on the bridge a couple of hours later. Pepper and I were trying on rings and bracelets and chains. Hal was way too cool for the kind of shop we were in (as in one we could actually afford), and he was two shops down wearing his cool shades and looking at watches that my dad would have to sell the house to be able to buy.

I didn't mind that Hal wasn't with us, and Mom and Dad were walking along the bridge looking into the water and holding hands (how embarrassing was that—they're my parents!). That meant Pepper and I could shop and try on stuff and smile at Italian boys without stupid comments from Hal and raised eyebrows from my dad.

Of course it was too good to last. Hal burst through the door of the shop just as a nice Italian man named Giuseppe was showing me this amazing chain with little stones in it that looked very expensive but wasn't (my favourite kind of jewellery).

"Check me out, ladies!" Hal wasn't walking; he was strutting like one of the doofus guys on that wrestling TV show that seems to be on twenty-four hours a day.

"What are we supposed to check out, Leonardo?" Pepper had been calling Hal Leonardo (after the painter, not the actor) ever since we'd left home.

Hal ignored her and walked up to me with his arm stretched out in front of him. On the wrist of that arm was a watch that even I had to admit was pretty spectacular.

"Wow," I breathed. I hated giving Hal credit for anything but what I was looking at wasn't your ordinary timepiece. The band was all bling-bling—lots of gold-looking shine—and the watch itself had more dials than the cockpit of an international jumbo jet. I'm pretty sure Hal had no idea what they were all for.

"Impressive." Pepper stared at the watch. "How much?"

Hal shrugged. "It's not about money, ladies. This beautiful piece of jewellery is a statement of who I am—an emerging artistic talent with a future. I need a timing device that fits that image."

Timing device?

"How much?" I repeated Pepper's question but I said it louder. I was afraid Hal had blown our spending budget for the entire trip on the first day.

Hal leaned his head toward me and looked around. "That's the best part. This is, like, a really expensive watch . . . and I got it for fifteen dollars. And I gave the guy an autograph."

"What guy?" I demanded.

"And who would want your autograph?" Pepper laughed.

"Well, okay, maybe he didn't know I was an artist. But when I told him that I was going to have one of my origi-nals hanging in the Uffizi Gallery, he seemed glad enough to have the autograph. Even dropped the price on the watch from twenty bucks to fifteen."

"Which place did you get it in?" I wanted to see what kind of loser would actually want my brother's autograph.

I hadn't seen Dad come into the shop. But suddenly he was there. Him and Mom. *Still* holding hands.

"What's up?" Dad looked at Hal, then at me, then at Hal again.

"Hal has a new watch," I said. I wasn't really ratting on my brother since I knew he was going to brag about it him-self. I hoped my tone of voice said it wasn't anything to brag about.

"Let's see." Dad and Mom looked at the watch as Hal held out his arm. He was still beaming at the brilliance of his purchase.

"And you paid how much for this?" Mom pulled Hal's wrist closer and stared hard at the watch.

"Fifteen bucks," Hal grinned. "I got the guy down. He wanted more."

"How much more?" Dad was shaking his head.

"He wanted twenty. I gave him fifteen and an autograph."

"Whose autograph . . . Babe Ruth's?"

Hal looked injured. "Mine."

"Hal, this watch is worth a lot of money. A *lot* of money," Dad was looking around. "Did you buy it in here?"

"I didn't get it in one of the shops." Hal didn't look quite as excited about his watch anymore. He was fidgeting a lot. "I . . . uh . . . bought it from a guy on the street. I came out of this one store and he—"

"Let's go. I want to see this bird." Dad had hold of Hal's arm and was pulling him out of the shop.

When we got outside Hal looked up and down the bridge. "I don't see the guy."

Dad looked around like he was hoping to spot some suspicious-looking character. After a minute he looked down at Hal.

"That brand is worth at least a couple of thousand dollars. Nobody sells that watch for fifteen bucks. Not even with an incredibly valuable autograph thrown in." I could hear the sarcasm in my dad's voice. And normally Dad isn't sarcastic. Pepper and me, yeah. Hal? All the time. But not Dad. That meant he was pretty upset.

"It was probably stolen. Or it's fake . . . which means it's worth even less than the fifteen dollars you paid for it."

I have to be honest. My brother's dumb, sometimes Hall-of-Fame dumb, but he's not dishonest. I mean, he'd lie to me about anything just because I'm his sister and that's what brothers do. But stealing? That's not Hal. I'm pretty sure it never occurred to him that he could be buying a hot watch.

"So what do I do?" Hal looked humbled for one of the few times in his life.

"I doubt if the culprits would steal it from around here and then sell it in the same place. It probably came from a store or someone's home in some other country. Or some other part of this country. If it is stolen, it'll be pretty much impossible to trace back to the owner. If it's fake, it doesn't matter. I guess you might as well wear it for now. But no more purchases from guys on the street, okay?"

"Okay. Hey, we should get a pizza. There's a place just down the bridge a ways."

One thing I'll say about my brother. He bounces back quickly from life's difficult moments.

5

Reception Deception

"Nice look," I told Hal.

We'd gone back to the hotel to change for the reception and Hal had just emerged from the bedroom wearing a T-shirt with a tie. A *necktie*.

The T-shirt was from a Tragically Hip concert and it had an image of the band on the front. The tie had a picture of Bugs Bunny and Homer Simpson sitting together in a convertible and waving.

"Thought you'd like it," Hal smiled at me.

"Are you going for the worst-dressed award?" Pepper giggled into her hand. "Don't they give those out at all these award things?"

Hal glared at her. "First of all, they only have those worst-dressed deals at the Academy Awards. I am an artist, not a mere actor."

I knew why he'd made that crack. Hal is aware that Pepper

wants to be a famous actress once her career as a teenage detective comes to an end.

"Second," Hal continued, "I am making a fashion statement here. People like me march to the drum of a different . . . uh . . . people like me walk to the marching of . . . uh . . . people like me—"

"Are losers." I finished the thought for Hal.

I noticed he had his new watch prominently displayed on his wrist. Part of the fashion statement, no doubt. Mom and Dad came out of their bedroom dressed like normal people and both of them looked at their son for a long time. Dad shook his head but apparently decided to let it go.

By the way, Pepper and I were wearing short summer dresses—mine had a pastel floral pattern and Pepper's was pink with white trim. We'd bought the dresses during our shopping trip. I was wearing white sandals and Pepper had these really nice flats on that almost perfectly matched her dress. We looked like people our age are supposed to look. Pepper looked really cute and I looked . . . okay.

I looked at Pepper and I knew she was thinking the same thing I was. No matter what happened, we had to make sure no one thought we were actually *with* Hal.

That was harder than we thought since the first thing that happened once we got to the Uffizi Gallery was the picture-taking session. All of the artists and their families were taken aside for photos.

When it was our turn, Pepper shook her head and I said, "I'm good, thanks," but Mom and Dad wouldn't let us off the hook. We stood and smiled (sort of) while photographers snapped away like crazy.

Then we were taken on a tour of the gallery. Now that part was cool. I didn't really know much about art, but we had studied the Renaissance in Social the year before so I'd actually heard of some of the famous Italian masters.

Which made it pretty amazing when I was standing before paintings by people like Raphael, Leonardo da Vinci and Michelangelo. I didn't want this part of the day to end. But, of course, it had to. Eventually our guide, a man named Antonio (it looked to me like Pepper was more interested in Antonio than the art he was showing us), told us we should return to the Sun Salon downstairs where the contest winners' works would be on display. Hal pretty much sprinted to the front of the group and Mom, Dad and Pepper followed, leaving me at the back of the group trying to catch one last glimpse of some of the paintings by the artists of a few hundred years ago.

That's when it happened. I was looking at a painting by someone named Caravecchio. The plaque nearby said he had lived in Siena in the fifteenth century and had died tragically in a rockslide. This was his only painting in the Uffizi.

But it wasn't the plaque that got my attention. It was the painting itself. It was of horses grazing in a beautiful sloping pasture. I stared at it for a long time, which I guess is what I do every time I see a painting or even a photograph of horses.

In the background, there was a building that looked like a barn. Next to it stood a house, a couple of storeys high with a balcony on the second storey. And on that balcony, looking out at the horses, was a man. An old man in a red shirt. I know this sounds ridiculous but I was sure this man was the same guy who had been in Hal's painting—the one who had disappeared.

Which, of course, was impossible. I *knew* that. And yet the more I looked at the painting the more convinced I was that this was the same guy. And remember how the other guy was pointing? Yeah, well, this one was pointing too—this time past the horses toward a village that you could just see off in the distance. I stared at the man for a long time and as I did I realized he wasn't looking at the horses at all. He was looking over their heads and just like the disappearing man in Hal's picture, he was looking straight ahead—right at me!

There are times when I can run fairly fast. No, not fairly fast—really fast. This was one of those times. The group had worked its way downstairs and was about to enter the Sun Salon. I went down the stairs two at a time. I think I was probably a bit noisy. I remember thinking how beautiful the staircase would have been if only I'd had time to enjoy it.

As my parents, my brother and my best friend started through the ornate double doors into the Sun Salon, I arrived to walk in beside them. Out of breath and maybe even a little sweaty. But there I was.

I fell in alongside Pepper. As soon as I caught my breath, I leaned as close to her as I could and whispered,

"First chance we get, I need you to follow me. There's something I have to show you."

"What?"

I shook my head. I knew that the answer to that question would take some time.

"Where?"

I pointed back over my shoulder with my thumb. "Upstairs."

"We can't sneak out during your brother's big moment," Pepper hissed at me. "Your parents will kill us."

It was a good point but we'd have to risk it.

"Mys-ter-y." I whispered the syllables like I was talking to a three-year-old.

"Say no more." Pepper grinned. "Just give me a nod and we're outta here."

I knew the "m" word would motivate Pepper. What bugged me was that I had exactly zero interest in getting caught up in something that might be even remotely mysterious. Yet here I was dragging my best friend—the second coming of Nancy Drew—off to check out something that was, to say the least, puzzling.

As we stood and listened to the speeches, I looked around the salon. The furniture in this room—from the elaborate little tables that were here and there, to the lamps, which were turned on even though it was daytime, to the cloth-covered chairs that people were sitting in or lounging against—looked really old and really expensive. The chair cushions had strips of gold thread running through the red cloth! I thought I'd kill to have one of those in my bedroom at home. Not that I'd actually let anyone sit on it—not my friends and definitely not Hal. It would be cool just to let them look at it . . . and admire how rich I was.

A man had stepped to the microphone that was set up at one end of the room. After he introduced himself as Bruno Gerusenti, one of the competition organizers, he told the crowd (in Italian and English) about the contest, and how the winners were selected.

Dad leaned down and whispered. "This is very impressive. I Googled him before we left home. Signore Gerusenti is considered the greatest living authority on Renaissance art. To have him doing this is amazing. This is huge for your brother."

Yeah, huge. I felt a wave of jealousy sweep over me again. I tried to fight it off by concentrating on what Signore Gerusenti was saying. (By the way, in Italy "Signore" is pronounced "seen-your.") Most of what he was saying was about the wonderful gifts each of these artists possess. Exactly the stuff you'd expect to hear. Exactly the stuff you didn't want to hear about your rotten little brother.

Then he started to introduce the winning artists. I figured this might be a good time for Pepper and me to escape the festivities.

I looked in Pepper's direction and jerked my head to show her what I was thinking. I jerked my head again. Pepper was looking right at me but I was getting no response. Not a nod, not a wink, not even a shrug—nothing. I jerked my head so many times I felt like one of Hal's bobblehead dolls . That's when I figured out that Pepper wasn't looking *at* me at all. She was looking *past* me.

I turned and followed her gaze. It took me about a nanosecond to figure out what had happened. Right behind me was this guy that I figured had to be one of the winning artists. And he was gorgeous. About fifteen, maybe sixteen, blond hair, tall, an amazing smile, very blue eyes. . . . I could almost understand the pathetic love looks Pepper was sending in his direction.

But there wasn't time for Pepper to fall in love at this exact moment. We had things to do. I looked back at her. *Yeah, good luck with that.* I moved to put myself between Pepper and the blond hunk, you know, to block her view. She moved. Then I moved. Then she moved. Then I moved. You get the picture.

Finally I grabbed her arm and mouthed, "Come on." She sort of focused on me and I started to lead her back toward the double doors. Just then, Signor Gerusenti said into the microphone, "Our first winner, from Copenhagen, Denmark, is Lars-Erik Jensen." Guess who Lars-Erik just happened to be? Uh-huh. Blue eyes, blond hair, the very one. There was no way in the world I was going to get Pepper out of that room now.

As it turned out, Pepper's instant crush saved us a lot of grief. One of the first things the organizers did with Lars-Erik was to have him and all of the members of his family gather in front of his painting for more picture taking. (By the way, Lars-Erik's painting was of these skaters on a frozen lake and it was, like, amazing.)

Anyway, I figured we better hang around until Hal was introduced. We'd have had major explaining to do if the family had been called forward for pictures and we weren't there.

Luckily we didn't have to wait long. Hal was the fourth artist introduced. After Lars-Erik, Signore Gerusenti introduced a really young female artist from Africa (she was even younger than Hal, and her painting, which blew everybody away, was of a mother elephant and her baby by a watering hole). Next came an Italian guy, first name Roberto. As far as I was concerned, he wasn't far behind Lars-Erik in the omigod-he's-gorgeous department. His painting was of a street at night and some people walking and talking. And a man and a woman were kissing under a streetlamp. Oh, yes, Roberto!

Hal was Hal. In other words, he embarrassed us all. When his name was called he high-fived all the Uffizi Gallery executives, except one really old lady who we found out later was a major financial contributor to the gallery. Hal *kissed* her. On the mouth. Except it wasn't romantic like in Roberto's painting, or even funny. It was just . . . gross. The old lady wiped her mouth with a very expensive looking embroidered handkerchief.

Then Hal made a speech. No other artist made a speech. Just my brother. The speech went like this: "I'd just like to say that it's, like, really great to have my picture hanging in this here Yafoozy Gallery right along with all the other great artists; guys like Mike Angelo, Leo and me. Speaking of pictures, I brought along some photos of myself, which I'll be happy to autograph and sell really reasonable." Then he looked over at the old lady—the one he'd kissed and who was still dabbing at her lips with the handkerchief. "I imagine you'll want one, eh, babe?"

There was more to Hal's speech but I had stopped paying attention. By that point, I'd worked my way into a corner behind some people and was looking for something to kill myself with. Then came the picture taking: Hal and his family. As I was slowly walking to the front of the room, I wondered about that whole family thing. How was it that I was the one to get stuck with a little brother like Hal? Had I done something when I was two years old to offend whoever's in charge of distributing little brothers? Did my mother have a fling with someone who worked in a carnival? Had there been some horrible mistake? Was my brother actually supposed to be raised by a family of chimpanzees in Tanganyika?

As the cameras clicked and whirred, I'm pretty sure the expression on my face was the "somebody help me!" one I had perfected after years of living in the same house with this cross between Homer Simpson and Don Cherry. The weird part was when I glanced over at Mom and saw that she had the same expression.

Five seconds after the picture taking was over (okay,

maybe ten seconds), I grabbed Pepper and dragged her back up the stairs. "Chris, will you let go! I was just about to introduce myself to Lars-Erik. I think he could be *the one*."

I kept dragging and finally she quit pulling back. "What do you *want*?" she asked in a very loud voice.

"There's something you have to see."

"Oh, yeah! The mystery." Now the roles were reversed and she was practically dragging me. Except she didn't know where we were going. Problem was . . . neither did I. There were dozens of rooms up on the second floor and I couldn't remember which one the Caravecchio painting was in. We dashed into a couple of different rooms and then a third. I was about to turn from that one as well when I noticed two people. They were standing off to one side of the room and the painting—the one I wanted to check out—was on the wall behind them. The couple—a man and a woman—didn't look like the sort of people who would spend a lot of time in galleries and museums. They looked hard . . . mean . . . sleazy. I guess hard, mean, sleazy people sometimes go to museums and stuff, but these two were just wrong for that place.

They stared at us. *Glared* is probably a better description.

And they were pointing, sort of in our direction. But maybe I was imagining that part. I had to admit the whole thing with the guy in—and then *not* in—Hal's painting was doing things to my brain.

Still, the two people in the corner of that room were doing a lot of whispering. I wasn't imagining *that*. Very energetic whispering. I didn't really want to take Pepper over to the horse painting with them standing right there so I gestured to her and we hung back by the entrance. I tried to look casual. Pepper just looked impatient. After we'd been standing there for a while I changed my approach. I stared right back at the two nasty-looking types hoping I'd force them to look away. And *go* away.

It didn't work. I thought again about how out of place they seemed in one of the most famous art galleries in the world. Not that you have to be rich or important to like art. But that was just it. They didn't look like people who would appreciate art at all.

In fact, they looked more like the kind of people you'd see in a police lineup. Especially the woman. She was taller than the guy—who was wearing jeans and a T-shirt, neither of which looked as if it was on a first-name basis with a washing machine—and she had curly black hair that looked like it had been glued onto the top of her head, then run over with an iron to squish it down. She was wearing a pantsuit that might have been in fashion before Pepper and I were born. It was black, like the rest of her ensemble—shawl, hat that looked like an upside-down soup pot without the handle and shoes. The shoes were runners and yes, they were black. When she finally turned a little in our direction I saw a pockmarked face, thin lips and little shark teeth that made her look like someone you wouldn't want mad at you. When she turned the rest of the way around, she looked *extremely* mad at us.

She slugged the guy on the arm and pointed. This time I was sure of it. She was definitely pointing at us. It was starting to seem like Italian people did a lot of pointing.

The man's eyes, which weren't all that big to start with, narrowed to paper-thin slits. For a minute, we all just stood there, staring at each other. Then, finally, the Dynamic Duo moved toward the door. As Shark Teeth and her husband/assistant/bodyguard (take your pick, although if anyone was a bodyguard in that twosome I would have bet on Shark Teeth) went by us on their way out of the salon, she gave us a look as black as her ensemble.

"Nice folks," Pepper said when we were sure they were out of hearing range.

"Yeah," I agreed, "but we haven't got time for that right now."

I led her to the painting, the one by Caravecchio. "What do you see?" As Pepper bent forward to take a closer look I alternated between watching her and looking over my shoulder to make sure that no one else was coming into the salon. I deliberately did not look at the painting so I wouldn't influence Pepper in any way.

"Horses?"

"Besides horses."

"Grass . . . pasture?"

"Besides pasture."

"Well, there's a barn."

"Right," I nodded. "And next to the barn . . . "

"A house."

"Now we're getting somewhere," I told her. "Is there a balcony on the house?"

"Uh-huh . . . on the second floor."

"And who is on the balcony?"

She leaned further forward. Silence.

"I said, who is on the balcony? Do you see the man on the balcony?"

"Chris, there's no one on the balcony. There are no people in the whole painting."

I finally looked at the painting. Then I looked again. Pepper was right. The man, the one who had been in the painting before, was not there. He'd disappeared just like the guy in Hal's painting. I was starting to really hate balconies.

I stood looking at the painting for a long time. Then I stepped back and looked at other paintings thinking maybe I had the wrong one.

But, of course, I didn't have the wrong one. Could I have imagined the man in the painting? Twice? In two different paintings? Was I losing my mind?

"Uh, listen, Chris, this is really interesting and everything but we really should get back down to the reception. I don't want us to look rude."

Yeah, right. I knew that Pepper's wanting to get back downstairs had nothing to do with being polite and everything to do with a cute Danish hunk named Lars-Erik.

"Pepper, there's something totally weird happening here. I saw a man pointing in Hal's painting and he's not there now. Then I saw the same man pointing in this painting and he's gone too. And those two nasty-looking characters were in this same room. Then they took off when they saw us. You don't see anything odd here?"

"What were the guys in the paintings pointing at?"

"I don't know ... I mean, the first guy, it was like he was pointing up the street and the second guy ..." I looked at the painting again, "the one who was standing right there, he was pointing off in that direction, I don't know, at something off in the distance, maybe that village."

I couldn't believe that I was trying to talk Pepper into the fact that there just might be some mysterious stuff happening here. Usually she's the one doing the convincing about some mystery she wants me to help her solve.

"Stress."

That's all she said.

"What?"

"It's stress." Pepper nodded knowingly, like she was an expert. "You've just learned that your brother has an amazing talent and you don't and it's gotten to you. Stress is like that. Some people faint. Some get all tired and shaky, you ... well, you see stuff that isn't there. It's nothing to be ashamed of."

Now I *was* stressed.

"First of all, the fact that my brother has talent for something doesn't bother me. It surprises me, but it doesn't bother me. Second, hello, I have talent too ... sort of. And three, I'm not seeing things that aren't there. Those men were in those paintings and they aren't there now. And if it wasn't for your stupid hormones and how you're all ga-ga over a guy with blond hair, blue eyes and an incredible body, you'd see that this is a mystery and you might even help me try to solve it instead of standing there sounding like Dr. Phyllis."

"Who's Dr. Phyllis?"

"It was a joke. Dr. Phil . . . Dr. Phyllis . . . get it?"

"No." Pepper patted me on the top of the head (I hate that!). "We'll talk about it later, Chris. Honest. But right now I think we better get our backsides down those stairs before somebody notices we're gone. Besides, I'd hate to miss it if Hal starts making out with the old lady again." She giggled and disappeared out the door and down the stairs.

I followed, trying to decide what was worse: people showing up and then disappearing from paintings; the fact that I was the only one who saw these people; my best friend thinking I was losing it; or my brother planting another one on his "babe."

I was actually laughing as I went down the stairs behind Pepper.

The Disappearing Artist

The next two days went the way days are supposed to go when people are on holidays. There was lots of sightseeing, (the Leaning Tower of Pisa really does lean—in fact, it looks like it could fall down at any minute—and the famous statue of David is seventeen feet high and he's . . . uh . . . naked), some very cool restaurants, castles, ancient ruins, beautiful churches and art, lots of art. (Did I mention the statue of David?)

I'd never really thought about the statues and paintings of the great Italian masters before, but when you are standing right in front of something that was actually created by, say, Michelangelo, it's very cool.

Even my brother, the cretin, was taking it all in. I just discovered that word (cretin) in a book the other day and believe me it's the perfect word to describe Hal. Look it up and I'll bet you agree.

But my favourite part of that two days was a drive we took out into the Tuscan countryside. Tuscany is the province in Italy where Florence and Pisa and Siena are located—sort of like Toronto and Ottawa are in Ontario or Los Angeles and San Francisco are in California.

The Blitzers, my parents' friends, drove us to a place called Maremma. They have cowboys there. I swear—cowboys! They don't look quite like our cowboys but they're the real deal, Italian style. Their hats are different, not normal cowboy hats. Instead they wear what are called fedoras—sort of like people wore in those old detective movies my mom and dad watch whenever they can get the remote out of my brother's hands. We saw the cowboys riding big, sturdy Maremmano horses, herding long-horned Maremmano bulls. We watched them for quite a while. Then we drove to a beach on the shores of the Tyrrhenian Sea.

For a while I was actually able to forget about the weird stuff that was happening in my life—like the disappearing guy in the paintings and how he seemed to be signalling me. I sprawled out on a blanket on the sand and spent a couple of hours reading a book I'd started on the plane. It's called *Bud, Not Buddy* and it's, like, one of my favourite books ever.

The sun made me sleepy after a while and I was actually dozing when I was shaken awake—never my favourite way to wake up. I was still in that fuzzy not sleeping but not really awake kind of headspace when Pepper's words got rid of the fuzzies. In a hurry.

"Chris, we've got to get back to Florence right away!" Her voice was shrill and I knew she wasn't messing around.

Hal heard her too. "Wazup?" Hal is into whatever dialogue he's heard on TV or in a movie or in something that he thinks is cool. *Wazup* was one of his latest.

Pepper ignored him and looked at me. "There's a message on my cellphone. Lars-Erik has been kidnapped!"

I sat up and looked back at her.

"Wow," Hal breathed.

"Whoa, wait a minute," I held up my hands. "How do you know?"

"Because it's him. He called me. " She passed me her cellphone. "Listen."

I gave her an, *oh, yeah, so you were able to exchange phone numbers with the Great Dane already* look, but Pepper wasn't paying attention.

I took the phone, pressed 4 to get the message again and held it to my ear. All I heard at first was panting, like someone trying to catch his breath . . . or who was maybe scared. "Pepper . . . Pepper . . . I . . . your number is the one I have from my speed dial pressed . . . I . . . Lars-Erik . . . I need . . . help . . . two people . . . they have . . . they have . . . grabbed me and pushed me . . . into their motor car . . . and we are . . . "

That was all. I handed the phone back to Pepper and she listened to the message again. Then I did the same thing. Then we looked at each other, both of us thinking like crazy.

"Is there any chance he's goofing around, that this is some kind of joke?"

"Come on, ladies, wazup?" Hal's shrill, irritating voice pierced our concentration.

Pepper ignored him and shook her head. "I don't think so. I mean, I hardly know the guy. We've talked on the phone a couple of times since the reception but that's it. I don't think someone would make a call like this as a joke."

"What, he phoned you up and said he was being kidnapped?" Hal again. "That's hilarious. I love that guy."

I nodded toward the phone. "Let him listen," I told Pepper. "Another opinion might not be a bad thing right now."

Pepper looked doubtful but she passed Hal the phone.

"Press 4," I said.

"Hello, I think I know that." Hal listened, then played the message again. As he did, his face went from big grin to surprise to downright serious. He handed the phone back to Pepper.

"Either that guy is an amazing actor or that's the real deal," Hal said. "I think something was going on when he made that call."

"And he wasn't able to finish—"

"Because the two people that he mentions in the call saw him or heard him and got the phone away from him." I finished Pepper's thought for her.

"Why would someone kidnap Lars-Erik?" Pepper stood up and brushed sand off her legs.

I shrugged and got to my feet. "I don't know."

"Maybe his family's, like, really rich." Hal suggested.

I nodded. "Yeah, it could be about ransom."

"Or they're important, like government or . . . maybe they're royalty."

Pepper started walking. "So what do we do?"

"Why don't you call his cellphone . . . maybe he got away or maybe if he was kidding around . . . "

"Good idea." Pepper made the call and Hal and I got our faces as close to the phone as we could.

"Lars-Erik? . . . Lars-Erik?"

I couldn't hear what, if anything, was being said so I just watched Pepper's face. Someone must have answered the phone or she wouldn't have been saying Lars-Erik's name. Pepper's facial expression changed even faster than Hal's had. It went from hopeful to angry. "Yeah, well, you know where you can—" She looked at me. "He hung up."

"Lars-Erik?"

"Someone else. A real creepy-sounding guy with an accent. I'm not even sure I got what he said. Something like . . . *your friend cannot be found.* Then I didn't get the next part, and the last part sounded like a bunch of foreign words and then *the others.* And that was it."

"We have to tell Mom and Dad and the police. We've got to report this right away." This was one of the first times my parents had been around as one of our mysteries began to unfold. I figured we'd better let them know what was going on.

"Maybe this is a case for Salt and Pepper and the amazing little brother." Hal was back to grinning.

"Hal, this isn't funny. And it definitely isn't about Salt and Pepper, so get that thought out of your head." I started running toward Mom and Dad, who were sitting on a couple of lawn chairs drinking San Pellegrino.

They listened to the message and we told them about Pepper calling Lars-Erik's number. Dad went off to find a policeman. He came back a few minutes later accompanied by a very large Italian cop with a very red face.

The policeman spoke English well and totally understood what we were telling him. He also listened to the message and then phoned into police headquarters in Florence. He told us we should report as soon as possible to an Inspector Rebussiani. He gave Dad the address. He also said we should take the phone to this Inspector Rebussiani right away.

"He is the smartest policeman in all of Italy," the red-faced constable said.

"I'm sure they have some things they can do to try to detect background noise in order to find where the kidnapping, if that's what it was, took place," said Dad. "I think we'd better go back right now."

Dad didn't get an argument from any of us and in a few minutes we were in the car and speeding back toward Florence.

So much for a quiet day at the beach.

7

Shark Teeth and Friend

By the time we got to the police station, Inspector Rebussiani had Lars-Erik's mom and dad in the office with him. They didn't look like royalty or even like people who were terribly important. Mostly they looked like people who were worried about their son.

The inspector gestured to someone in an outer office who brought more chairs and eventually we were all seated, looking at each other and worrying.

"I assume you all know one other, at least slightly." Inspector Rebussiani spoke in a booming voice that had almost no accent.

We all nodded to him and to each other.

"I have spoken at length with the Jensens and they have no idea why anyone would want to abduct their son. Lars-Erik went out for a walk and, as you know, did not return."

He looked at Pepper and me. "Which of you young ladies received the call?"

"I did," Pepper said and handed the phone across the desk.

The inspector listened to the call, then handed the phone to the Jensens. "I need you to listen to this message and identify the voice for me."

First Mr. Jensen listened to the message, then Mrs. Jensen did the same. When she handed the phone back to Inspector Rebussiani, there were tears in her eyes.

"That is the voice of Lars-Erik," Mr. Jensen said softly.

"Lars-Erik," Mrs. Jensen nodded and repeated in a still softer voice.

Inspector Rebussiani turned to us. "Do any of you have any idea why someone might kidnap Lars-Erik?"

All of us looked at each other and shook our heads.

"Inspector," Mr. Jensen leaned forward in his chair. He looked about the same age as my dad but had Lars-Erik's hair and facial features. A nice-looking man. "Why would this be done? Kidnap my son, it is not possible, no reason could there be . . . "

"I don't know, sir, why this has happened." Inspector Rebussiani was a big man, a tough-looking guy, but he spoke very gently now as he looked at the Jensens. "I promise you we will spare no effort to discover who has committed this crime. Ransom is a possibility. But there are others too: mistaken identity, even a prank, a cruel one to be sure. We just don't know. When we learn that, it may give us some idea as to who is involved. That's what we want to find out. And I repeat, we will spare no effort in doing so. The minute we know something we will let you know."

Mr. Jensen nodded, sat back in his chair and put his arm around his wife, who was crying quietly into a handkerchief.

"What about you … Pepper, is it?" Inspector Rebussiani turned his attention to my best friend. "You seem to have known the young man better than the others in your group."

"I guess a little better. I talked to him a bit at the reception."

"And you exchanged phone numbers."

Pepper's cheeks turned the colour of a prairie fire. "Uh … yeah."

"And you've spoken to him on the phone."

"A couple of times," Pepper nodded.

"In these conversations did he sound worried? Did he say anything about thinking he was being followed or anything?"

"No, he sounded fine. I mean I don't know him that well but he sounded … uh … fine."

"She means hot," Hal said.

Pepper's cheeks got brighter still.

"Hot?" Inspector Rebussiani repeated. "As in temperature?"

Hal shook his head. "Hot as in *ooh, you're such a hunk.*"

Pepper had a coughing attack, Dad glared at Hal and I thought I saw a tiny smile form at the corners of the inspector's mouth.

"That reminds me," Inspector Rebussiani turned back to the Jensens, "you did bring a picture?"

Mr. Jensen nodded and handed a photo to the inspector. Hal looked like he had something to say but he changed his mind. Probably a good thing if he was hoping to live long enough to, say, reach puberty.

"I'll circulate this both here in Florence and in the neighbouring areas. And I'll need to keep your phone," the inspector told Pepper, "but I'll arrange to get you another with the same number. In case Lars-Erik is able to call you. And, of course, if that should happen, I'll expect to hear from you right away."

Pepper nodded enthusiastically.

"That goes for everyone. If any of you should think of something that might help or if you are contacted by anyone, you can reach me at any hour. Please do so."

There was nodding and "Yes, sirs" all around the room.

"One more thing." The inspector was looking at me now. "I understand you two have been fairly successful amateur detectives—"

Hal was clearing his throat like crazy.

"Excuse me," the inspector said, "you *three*. That's very nice and I'm very impressed but this is serious business and it would be best handled by the police. Are we clear on that?"

"Yes, sir," I said and meant it.

Inspector Rebussiani stood up and passed out business cards to all of us, indicating the meeting was over. We all got up to leave. My dad took a step forward and held out his hand. "Anything we can do, Inspector, believe me, we'll be happy to help. By the way, you speak excellent English, almost no accent. You are . . . ?"

"Italian." Inspector Rebussiani smiled and shook my dad's hand. "Born and bred. But I attended the University in Edinburgh, Scotland."

"Ah, I thought something like that."

"One last thing," the inspector said, "and it's totally unrelated to this case but I wanted to mention it. There's a gang of low-level crooks operating in this area. They're selling cheap knockoffs of watches and other jewellery. The watches have big-name brands on them and they look like the real thing to the untrained eye but they're worth a couple of bucks at the most. I probably don't even need to mention it since you all look much too smart to fall for something like that but all the same—fair warning."

I looked over at Hal. He had put his hand behind his back and was trying to pretend he had an itch that needed immediate attention. Pepper and I looked at each other and even with all the serious stuff with kidnappings and everything, it was all we could do to keep from laughing out loud.

We waited while one of the officers arranged for another phone to be delivered to Pepper. It didn't take long. Outside on the street, it seemed somehow even hotter than it had been in the earlier part of the day.

My mom and dad and the Jensens decided go down the street to a little café. They thought it would be good for Mrs. Jensen to have a cup of tea.

"You three are welcome to join us."

"Thanks, Dad, but I think we'll go for a walk or something," I said. I didn't think we'd be up to adult conversation or tea just now.

We walked. Aimlessly at first. Then I realized that it seemed as if Pepper was leading us in a certain direction.

"Have you got somewhere particular in mind?" I asked her.

She nodded. "Lars-Erik and I were going to meet at this park called Boboli Gardens. We were supposed to be there in about a half hour. I thought maybe we could head over there even though ... "

"How was the meeting in the park supposed to happen when we were going to be sightseeing and sunbathing all day?"

"We ... uh ... sort of set up this place where we'd go every day at the same time if we could. And if one of us couldn't be there, the other one would understand and we'd just try again the next day."

I stared at her with my mouth open. "And I thought Mom and Dad and all their little romantic moments were painful. How did you get all this organized?"

Pepper held up her cellphone. I nodded.

"So, are we going or not?" she asked.

"Can't do any harm," I said. "Shut up, Hal."

I could see my brother was about to say something that he thought would be outrageously funny and I didn't think Pepper needed that right now. She looked kind of shaken up even though it was true that she hardly knew Lars-Erik.

We got to the Boboli Gardens and for a while walked around in silence. Even with the crisis going on, it was hard not to be amazed by the beauty of the city. There were amazing sculptures in the park (my favourite was called Neptune Spearing Fish) and beautifully kept hedges and flowerbeds everywhere. The hedges were all trimmed into geometric patterns. There were wild, more natural areas, too, with groves of ilex and cypress trees.

Pepper didn't seem to notice any of it. I couldn't blame her. Hal didn't notice either, but that was just Hal. If the park had been full of really gross stuff, now that would have gotten my brother's attention.

We sat down on a park bench and all three of us were quiet for a couple of minutes.

That's when I remembered. "Jeez, I forgot to tell the inspector about those two people we saw at the Uffizi."

"What two people?" Hal asked.

"Pepper and I saw these two nasty-looking people at the gallery the day of the reception. *Really* nasty. A man and a woman. They were acting sort of suspiciously. You wouldn't have seen them because you were busy kissing old ladies." I thought that last part might cheer Pepper up, but she didn't smile. "Besides, they were upstairs."

"Upstairs?"

"Yeah."

"You mean you were upstairs while the reception was

going on? While your own brother was being honoured for his brilliance?"

"Don't worry, we didn't miss your speech."

"I wish we had." That was Pepper. Maybe she was getting back to normal.

"I hardly remember those people," Pepper said. "You think they could be the kidnappers?"

I shrugged. "I'm not sure at all. But the inspector said to let him know if we thought of anything that might be useful. I'd better phone him. Let me have your cell."

"Okay, but make it fast. In case Lars-Erik is trying to call."

"Right." I took the phone and walked a little way away from them so I wouldn't have to listen to Hal making comments during my conversation with Inspector Rebussiani.

I reached him right away and relayed our encounter with the two grumpy people at the gallery. He sounded a little mad that I hadn't mentioned it at the meeting but when I told him I'd forgotten all about it he seemed okay. I described the two people as best I could. The inspector thanked me and hung up the phone. When I got back to the bench Pepper was chewing on a fingernail and Hal was walking back and forth behind her.

"Well, this is fun." He used his totally bored voice.

"Why don't you go buy a nice watch or something?" Pepper glared at Hal.

"And why don't you—"

"Whoa, wait a minute." I cut him off. "Speak of the devil . . . devils."

"Huh?"

"What are you talking about?"

I sat back down beside Pepper. "Okay, don't anybody be obvious about it, but over there, in those trees, I'm positive those two people—the grumpy ones from the Uffizi—are watching us."

"Which direction?"

"Six o'clock. Over behind Hal. There's some cypress trees—the really tall ones. They're hiding in there."

"Six o'clock?" Hal blurted. "That's right in front of us."

"That's twelve o'clock, idiot," Pepper told him. "Six o'clock is behind us. I thought you watched television."

Pepper did a lot of stretching and what she must have thought was totally un-obvious shifting around to get a look. Hal bent down to tie his shoe and cranked his head around in the direction of the trees. Smooth.

"It's them. I remember them now," Pepper hissed at me.

"I say we rush 'em," said Hal. "I'll take the guy and you two handle the chick."

I ignored Hal and decided to risk a glance in their direction. They were still there and they were definitely watching us. And the woman—Shark Teeth—actually looked like she was snarling. But why?

"Yeah, I don't think the 'rushing 'em' program is a real good idea," I told Hal. "First of all, that guy would squish you like a bug and I'm pretty sure it might take more than Pepper and me to deal with Shark Teeth."

"Shark Teeth, that's good," Hal laughed.

"They're leaving," Pepper announced.

"After 'em," Hal leaped up.

Pepper's head was bobbing up and down. "We should at least follow them."

Oh no, here we go again. Salt and Pepper one more time. Another Chronicle in the making. Even as I thought that, I could see that it might be a good idea to do what Hal and Pepper were suggesting.

"Okay, but Pepper, you call Inspector Rebussiani and tell him what's going on here."

Five minutes later we'd lost them. We were just standing in the middle of the Piazza di San Giovanni, trying to look inconspicuous, when three cop cars came screaming up, making it look like we were international criminals or something. So much for inconspicuous.

Inspector Rebussiani climbed out of one of the cars and stood in front of us.

"We followed them this far . . . but they're gone," I wheezed. We'd been moving fast and I was kind of out of breath. "Maybe they ducked into one of these shops and out the back way. With all these people around it was kind of hard—"

"Which is why you'll leave the policing to us."

That made me angry. Pepper must have felt the same way.

"We're trying to help here," she said.

The inspector nodded and there was a hint of a smile. "And you did well. I appreciate it. I just want you to know that these could be dangerous people. Remember that. If they are the kidnappers or are connected in any way to the disappearance then . . . ." He stopped, kind of like he'd just thought of something.

"They were watching you, you said?"

"Uh-huh."

"Then if this isn't a coincidence, and I don't believe in coincidences, and if there is some connection between these two and what happened to Lars-Erik, then I think you three need to be very careful. Stay together. No one goes off alone. And stay out of remote areas. It's best to be where there are people around. I'll let your parents know."

I nodded, Pepper stared at the policeman and Hal scuffed the ground with the toe of one shoe.

"You think we could be targets, like they might try to kidnap one of us next?" Pepper asked.

"It's not impossible."

"Right," I said. "We'll be careful."

The inspector's cellphone rang and he turned away from us to answer it. His part of the conversation was in Italian so I didn't get any of it. When he turned back to us, he looked grim. "What I said a minute ago is more important now than ever."

"What do you mean?" I asked him.

"Another of the young artists is missing. A girl this

time. From Australia. Fourteen years old. She has been gone for a couple of hours. Her parents can't locate her. I have to go. Remember what I said."

And he was gone. I looked around, feeling a little paranoid. I didn't see any sign of Shark Teeth and her partner. And though the temperature was maybe 100 degrees Fahrenheit, I shivered.

The Legend of Caravecchio

"So what now?" Hal had his bare feet on the coffee table and was staring at his toes. "If we have to be with adults the rest of our time in Italy, I'm going to jump off the Ponte Vecchio."

He even pronounced the name of the bridge correctly, which was further proof of my theory that my brother was smarter than he let on. He liked people to believe he was dumb so he acted like he had Corn Flakes for brains. And he was pretty good at it.

"I'll be right beside you," Pepper grumbled.

"I am, like, totally bored," said Hal.

That wasn't good. A bored Hal usually meant some stupid practical joke with his older sister as a target for his sick humour.

"That isn't exactly what they said," I pointed out as I looked up from an Italian golf magazine. I don't play golf and I can't read Italian so that gives you a pretty fair idea just how exciting our lives were at that exact moment.

We were sitting in what we called the TV room of our suite at the hotel. The TV was on but the sound was down. Pepper was sort of looking at it but I could tell she wasn't very focused. Good thing since the program looked like a documentary on people who hand weave carpets. Fascinating.

"Yeah?" Hal looked over at me. "Well, that's what I heard. Oh, we can go for walks as long as it's during the day and we stay together. Me stuck with you two full-time. Now, that's what I call non-stop fun."

"Right back atcha, Swamp Breath." Pepper glared at him. "It's not like we want to spend a bunch of time bonding with you either. There's only so much information I need about baseball, your latest female sports star crush and of course, your favourite topic of conversation—the fart."

"Shut up, loser," Hal said.

"Nice comeback."

"Okay, you two." I looked at each of them in turn. "This isn't helping. We have to make the best of a crappy situation. We're only here for a few more days so let's try and get along. Besides, maybe Rebussiani will solve the case and find the missing kids and we'll be back to normal."

I wasn't nearly as optimistic as I tried to sound. The inspector had just left a few minutes before. He'd come by the hotel to ask a few more questions and update us on the case. The second missing kid's name was Rachel

Thompson. I remembered her from the reception. I'd guessed she was about the same age as Pepper and me, very pretty, long brown hair, tall, thin model's body—what I wished I looked like.

"Or maybe we could help him." Pepper stood up as she said it.

"Alright!" Hal was on his feet, too. "I'm all about crime-fighting."

"Forget it, both of you." I shook my head so hard I hurt my neck. "You heard the inspector. He doesn't need or want our crime-fighting abilities. And Mom and Dad will ground us for the next thirty years if we so much as—"

"We're already grounded." Hal waved his arm around the room. "In fact, this is worse. This is house arrest."

Hal loves his police-TV-show vocabulary.

"We've snuck out before, we can do it again." Pepper said. A few minutes before, she and Hal had been at each other's throats. Now, they were high-fiving each other. I thought I might hurl.

"No way," I raised my voice a decibel or two. "I'm not sneaking. I'm not detecting. I'm not—"

"We don't have to sneak," Pepper interrupted. "All we have to do is go for one of those walks like they gave us permission to do. Is it our fault if some clue happens to fall out of the sky and we have to investigate it?"

"Exactly right." Hal nodded agreement.

"Listen up, both of you—" I had planned to argue some more but for some reason the guy in Hal's painting popped into my head—the same guy that had been in the painting at the Uffizi, the same guy who had disappeared off the balcony in both pictures—and I guess I kind of changed my mind in mid-sentence.

"Okay, first of all, clues don't just, like, fall out of the sky. As a matter of fact, in this case there are no clues, other than Shark Teeth and her ugly pal. And we have no idea where to start looking for them. And even if we did, I don't think that would be a very smart idea. But there is one guy I'd like to talk to. He might not be able to help but maybe ... maybe ... "

———

Signore Gerusenti's office was impressive, to say the least. There were almost as many paintings on his walls as there were in each salon throughout the Uffizi. And not just any old paintings. Old *Masters*. I'm no expert but they looked like important pieces of art.

Unlike Inspector Rebussiani, Signore Gerusenti had a marked accent. When he spoke it sounded like, *why donna we havva summa pizza?* But I'm not going to write it like that so you'll just have to imagine the accent.

"It is good to see you young people again." He smiled across his desk at us. "And, of course, my talented young artist friend." He beamed at Hal. "There has been great interest in the display of works by all of the young artists."

"I guess you've heard about the two missing kids," I said.

"A terrible tragedy." Signore Gerusenti's face turned serious. "I can't imagine who would do such a thing. But I am confident in the abilities of our esteemed Inspector Rebussiani."

"Yeah ... uh, we are too," I agreed.

"You mentioned on the phone you wanted to ask me about something."

I'd phoned on our way to the gallery to make an appointment. I hadn't told Hal and Pepper why I suddenly wanted to talk to Signore Gerusenti. Well, actually I lied. I told them Signore Gerusenti was planning to feature Salt and Pepper and the talented Hal in an advertising campaign—lots of photos, maybe some personal appearances. I told them the advertising slogan was, "Where is the next generation of artists? It's a mystery." Then I made up some baloney about how Salt and Pepper and Hal were solving the mystery. Weak, I know, but I figured (with their egos!) that it might convince them. And it did.

But my real reason for wanting to see Signore Gerusenti had to do with my dad's comment that he was greatest living expert on Renaissance painting and painters. Maybe he might shed a little light on the disappearing man.

"How may I be of help?" Signore Gerusenti folded his hands across his chest.

For a few seconds I toyed with the idea of forgetting about the whole thing and just getting up and leaving. Then I thought about the two kidnapped kids and how there could be more if the kidnappers weren't caught.

And I told him the whole thing. About the guy in Hal's

painting, About the guy in the painting upstairs. And about how I seemed to be the only person who ever actually saw the guy. There was a lot of eye rolling from Hal and Pepper and a few threatening glares as they figured out there was no advertising campaign. There were even a few groans but I stuck with it to the end.

"I know it's weird but I keep thinking maybe the guy is trying to get some message to me and that maybe the message might have something to do with what's been happening to the kids from the competition." I looked hopefully at Signore Gerusenti.

He closed his eyes and didn't say anything for a long time. Hal yawned and Pepper shook her head. When Signore Gerusenti still hadn't said anything or even moved after a couple of minutes I started to think maybe he'd found my story totally boring and nodded off.

I wasn't the only one who thought so. Hal started making snoring noises and Pepper started fussing around like she was getting ready to leave.

Finally, Signore Gerusenti opened his eyes, shifted his shoulders around and unfolded his hands. Then he leaned forward and placed his hands on the desk.

"I am going to tell you a story," he said. "It is a kind of legend—one that is not often talked about, mostly, I suppose, because so few people believe it."

"Do you believe it, sir?"

Signore Gerusenti smiled but didn't answer the question. Instead he said, "The painting upstairs in which you saw the man on the balcony. Do you remember the name of the artist?"

"I think so," I said. "Cara ... Caravecchio—yeah that's it. I don't think I've ever heard of him before."

"Few have," Signore Gerusenti smiled. "He was not terribly famous but he was extremely influential and important. Many of our most famous Masters studied under Caravecchio. Caravecchio had a studio in a little village at the foot of some hills near here. Students would study and live there for months at a time, learning their craft from a man who was a genius. He could have been one of the greatest artists of all time but instead he devoted his life to teaching others. And they were the ones who would become the Italian Masters we still talk about several hundred years later."

Signore Gerusenti paused, took a handkerchief from his pocket and wiped his forehead. I looked over at Pepper and Hal. Pepper seemed at least a little interested in what he was saying. Hal was looking around but at least he wasn't interrupting, which was probably the best I could hope for.

Signore Gerusenti cleared his throat and smiled at the three of us. "But then came a day that all of us who care about Renaissance art will always celebrate. It was a hot summer day in 1492, the same year that Columbus is credited with discovering your continent. It had rained for many days prior, but that day, after the rain had stopped, there was a terrible mud and rock slide. The little studio was almost completely buried with all of the students

inside, seven in all. Caravecchio himself was out of the
building, having gone to a nearby well to fetch water for
the students to drink."

"Did any of them get out?" Hal asked. I glanced again at
him. Now he was as riveted on the story as Pepper and I.
He was leaning forward, hands on knees, his eyes wide
and waiting for more.

Signore Gerusenti nodded. "They all did. But only
because of Caravecchio. He ran back to the building and
like a madman he dug through the mud and debris, single-
handedly pulling away great wooden beams and massive
boulders. Eventually others arrived to help but all who
were there said it was the teacher who saved those children. One by one he pulled each of them to safety. Some
were badly injured, but all lived and recovered. We don't
know the names of the students who were trapped in the
slide but it is certain that at least one or two of them went
on to become people whose works hang in the greatest
galleries and museums in the world. Including this one."
He waved an arm to indicate the Uffizi.

For a couple of minutes we all sat in silence. "That's a
totally amazing story, sir, but I'm not sure how it helps us
with the disappearing guy in the paintings."

Signore Gerusenti smiled. "There is more. Minutes after
the last young man was pulled to safety, Caravecchio
clutched at his chest, fell to the ground and died. So great
was the strain of his effort that it had taken his life. But ... "
Signore Gerusenti paused again, like our teachers do when

they are about to make an important point or give the punchline of some dumb teacher joke.

"But," he repeated, "there are those who think that the great teacher's story did not end there. A few years ago, a busload of students were on their way to a summer art camp near Siena. Again there had been rain and fog and suddenly out of the fog, there appeared a man. He was wearing a red shirt and a cloth cap and he was pointing. He said not a word, merely stood in the road pointing. The bus driver stopped, of course, and was quite angry at this intrusion. He climbed down from the bus to scold the man. But the man would not move. Nor did he speak. He just pointed up the road. Finally the driver walked up the road a ways and around a bend. There, a bridge had been washed out. In the fog and the rain he would certainly have driven the bus into the raging river below. And when he returned to the bus to thank the man—"

"Let me guess," I said. "He was gone. Disappeared into thin air."

"Quite correct. And there have been other instances, always involving children and always with the man in the red shirt and cloth cap saving them from disaster, only by pointing."

Signore Gerusenti leaned forward in his chair and folded his hands on his desk. "Now it is time for me to ask you a question. The man in the paintings, the one you saw. What did he look like?"

I thought back. "He was old," I said, "not a very big

man, really, and he was wearing a red shirt and some kind of flat hat on his head."

Signore Gerusenti smiled again. "Then perhaps you have your answer. Or at least part of it. What we don't know, of course, is just what Caravecchio, if it was him, was pointing to. But we may have at least a clue."

"What clue?" Pepper asked. I was wondering the same thing. "If there's anything we could use right about now, it's a clue."

"The painting that you saw upstairs? In it, Caravecchio painted a pastoral scene, a farm with horses."

"That's right," I nodded.

"But what is perhaps important is that the farmhouse he painted was not far from Siena. Your painting," Signore Gerusenti looked at Hal, "... is of the Palio, one of the most famous horse races in the world. It takes place in—"

"Siena!" Pepper, Hal and I yelled it at the same time.

Signore Gerusenti held up his hands. "Wait. There is something else I must tell you. There are a great many people who do not believe the legend of Caravecchio. One of those with whom I have discussed this legend is Inspector Rebussiani. Perhaps because of his training, he finds it difficult to attach much importance to such stories. I tell you this only because you may be disappointed at his reaction when you tell him about this ... clue."

"Maybe we won't tell him." Hal stuck his chest out— the macho man. "Maybe we'll take care of this ourselves."

"Wrong," I shook my head. "Wrong, wrong, wrong.

There is absolutely no way we are getting any more involved in another mystery. We tell the inspector what we think about the paintings and we are out of it. Period."

"There's one part I don't get." Pepper was frowning the way she does when she's thinking hard. "The guy in the painting—this Caravecchio—you said he shows up sometimes and he saves kids. And you said he's always pointing. But in the twerp's painting and the one upstairs, the one Salt saw, what was he pointing at?"

It was Signore Gerusenti's turn to frown. "I am sorry. These words . . . *twerp* . . . *salt*, it is for food, no? I do not understand."

"Sorry, Sir," Pepper grinned. "Those are nicknames. Twerp is what we call Hal because he's a loser, dweeb, dork, pain in the butt, you know? A twerp."

"It's all about jealousy, Signore Gerusenti. They only wish they could be like me," Hal was sending dagger looks at Pepper.

Pepper ignored him. "And Salt is Christine's nickname. I guess we're sort of famous for solving mysteries. I'm Pepper and she's Salt. Especially when we're in the middle of trying to solve a mystery."

"Which we aren't," I said quickly but I got the feeling no one was listening.

"I see," Signore Gerusenti nodded in Pepper's direction. "To return to your question, it is a very good one, to be sure. And I am not sure I can answer it. Perhaps if we were to look at the two paintings and you could tell me exactly where Cara . . . uh . . . where the man was standing and where he was pointing, it might help."

Signore Gerusenti stood up, came around the desk and led us to the door. He opened it and started out, then stopped so suddenly that we all tumbled into him like characters in a Three Stooges movie.

He didn't seem to notice. "Ah, Paulo, I want you to meet my friends—Hal Bellamy, one of our young artists from the exhibition, his sister Christine and their friend, Pepper McKenzie. This is Paulo Paolini, my assistant. He was largely responsible for the competition. In fact, it was his idea—and a brilliant one at that."

Paulo looked uncomfortable with the praise and smiled shyly at each of us in turn.

I looked at Pepper. She was watching Paulo. Another good-looking guy.

"Hello," he said.

We said hi and started to move off.

"I have been telling these young people about Caravecchio," Signore Gerusenti told his assistant.

Paulo smiled again. "We must be careful about misleading visitors to our country," Paulo said. "Caravecchio was one of our lesser painters, but he seems determined to make his mark in other ways. Saving people, warning others, appearing here and there to point the way. It is a lovely idea but I would not read too much into signals one sees in paintings and so on. It is my very great honour to meet all of you. I wish you well."

Paulo moved away with one last smile. Signore Gerusenti turned to us. "My assistant's attitude represents the much more conventional view of the Caravecchio story. I'm afraid I'm one of the few who regards him as something more than an embarrassing historical footnote."

"Paulo seems really nice," Pepper said. No surprise there.

"How long has he been your assistant?" I asked.

"Only about a year. Paulo comes from one of Siena's richest families. Indeed he has a very lovely home there still. But he is determined to make his way in the world without the help of the family fortune. It is an admirable desire."

"Yes," I said as I watched Paulo disappear into what I guessed was his office a few doors away.

We set off, first for the upstairs room that held the Caravecchio painting. Pepper and Hal growled and hissed at each other all the way up the stairs and down the hall to the salon. Very junior high, which I told them. But they were too busy hating each other to pay any attention to me. I was glad Signore Gerusenti seemed so focused on getting to the salon that he didn't seem to notice my brother and my best friend being so juvenile. I was glad that when we got to the Caravecchio, Hal and Pepper had stopped sniping at one another and were staring at the scene Caravecchio had so carefully created. For a few seconds I was caught up in the beauty of the work and almost forgot why we were there. That pleasant feeling didn't last long.

Signore Gerusenti, too, was leaning forward, eyes intent on canvas. "If you could indicate where you saw the man standing." He looked quickly at me and then back at the painting.

"Right there." I pointed to the now empty balcony. "And he seemed to be pointing in that direction."

Signore Gerusenti looked at the spot I had pointed to but didn't say anything right away. Then he took a deep breath. "Many of us know the very place Caravecchio was depicting. It is in the country, north of Siena. And it would seem as though the man in the red shirt and cloth cap was pointing in the direction of the city itself."

"But, dude, why? What's the message?" Hal asked. A good question.

Signore Gerusenti shrugged slightly. "Perhaps we should look at your painting next."

A couple of minutes later we were standing in front of Hal's painting, giving it the same careful examination we had given the Caravecchio moments before. Again I pointed to where I'd seen the mysterious man and indicated the direction in which he'd been pointing.

Signore Gerusenti took even more time than usual before answering. He rubbed his jaw, stepped back, then closer again and finally removed his glasses. Then he looked at us.

"This, of course, is the Palio, and the race, as you know, takes place in Siena. I lived in Siena and studied there for a long time. If this is where you remember him being, he is pointing to a part of the city . . . I believe your word is *residential*. Many houses and small apartments."

"In other words, lots of places to hide kidnapped kids," Pepper said.

"Unfortunately, yes."

"He could have made the clues a little more definite," I complained.

"True." Signore Gerusenti nodded his head. "But if these are indeed messages designed to help to find the missing young people, than Caravecchio has done a very good job of narrowing down the area that should be searched."

I nodded. "But I have one more question. Why is it that I'm the only one who receives the messages? Why hasn't anyone else seen the man in the paintings?"

"I have been thinking upon that same question," Signore Gerusenti replied. "Perhaps it is because he is of the opinion that you are the one who will find the missing children. That you are the key to solving this mystery."

"Salt and Pepper ride again!" Pepper grinned.

"With the help of their daring young assistant." Hal was grinning, too.

Again with the grinning.

Guess who wasn't grinning. Yeah, that'd be me.

Outside on the street again we walked for a while— Hal and Pepper joking around, trading insults, making comments that made it sound like they weren't taking the Caravecchio story very seriously, me just thinking.

Finally Pepper seemed to notice. "Hey, what's up, Chris?"

"Did anybody else notice something a little bit strange about our conversation with Paulo, Signore Gerusenti's assistant?"

"Like what?" Hal looked at me.

"I noticed he was cute." Pepper smiled. That *would* be the thing Pepper would notice.

"None of us had said anything about Caravecchio giving us signs or signals in paintings, yet he made a point of telling us not to pay too much attention to what we saw in paintings. Why would he say that?"

Pepper shrugged. "Maybe Caravecchio was famous for doing that."

"Maybe, but Signore Gerusenti didn't say anything about that when he was telling us about the stuff Caravecchio has been doing since he's been . . . uh . . . dead."

"I think you've been reading too many mysteries," Hal snorted. "You're starting to suspect everyone. I thought he was a good guy."

"Yeah, you're probably right, both of you," I agreed, even though I didn't feel that way inside.

"Not *probably* right." Hal went back to grinning. "*Definitely* right. As always."

"So the key to this whole thing has to be Caravecchio." I looked up at the Italian sun as I said it.

"If you buy that whole legend thing," Pepper said.

"Dead guy shows up whenever kids need saving," Hal snorted. "You have to admit, it's a little hard to buy."

I didn't say anything. I didn't tell them that I bought it. I totally bought it.

9

Hal, the Idiot

Hal struck later that night. You'll recall that I figured we were about due for one of Hal's stupid practical jokes. I was right.

Pepper and I were in our room watching one of those Bourne movies. I'm not much of an action movie/spy thriller fan but Matt Damon sort of makes all the shooting and blowing stuff up worth it.

There was a knock on our bedroom door. Pepper and I looked at each other. I was a little nervous to answer it. I figured it was probably Mom or Dad or maybe Hal coming over to bug us. But what if it wasn't them? Somebody out there somewhere was kidnapping kids. And here we were sitting in a hotel room by ourselves with only Matt Damon on a 36-inch flat screen to protect us.

I tiptoed over to the door and pressed my ear to the oak finish. I couldn't hear anything.

"Hello?" I called out. "Who's there?"

No answer.

I looked over at Pepper. "Well?"

"We won't find out if we don't open the door," she shrugged.

I opened it a crack and tried to see who or what was out there. I saw exactly nothing. I couldn't hear anything either so I figured whoever had knocked was gone. I opened the door wide.

And there it was.

"It" was a room service tray—one of those fancy silver things on wheels. This one had a nice white cloth covering it and on the cloth instead of food was . . . a painting. It was huge—as big as some of the paintings in the Uffizi—and it was propped up on the room service cart at an angle facing partly toward us and partly down the hall. It took me about one and a half seconds to figure out who the artist was. The painting was of two girls—guess which two? One of them was struggling to lift this gigantic bra, and judging from the effort she was making—the bra was, like, major heavy, like it was made of cement. There was sweat on her forehead and she was gasping for air as she tried to lift the thing, which actually looked like you could get major boulders into each of the cups.

That girl was me. It was pretty obvious. I think I mentioned that I'm . . . uh . . . still working on that whole figure thing and to be honest, I'd have to say there hasn't been a whole lot happening in that department. Obviously Hal had noticed and this was his not-so-funny way of pointing out my . . . um . . . shortcomings. My sicko little brother had used the underwear theme for some of his stupid jokes before. As I looked at the picture I could hear laughing behind me. Pepper obviously agreed with Hal that this was pretty funny stuff. That's when I focused on the other person in the painting. She was standing behind me trying to read an instruction manual titled, *Things I Don't Need.*

It was hard to read the title since the book was upside down. The look on Pepper's face announced to the world that she was either dumb or illiterate or both. Pepper stopped laughing. I figured she must have seen that part of the painting.

I had to admit Hal had done a pretty good job of making the two girls look a lot like Pepper and me—even with the brown-haired girl's face straining as she tried to lift the bra from hell and the redhead looking like a spaced-out loser from Dumbo High.

But the worst part was that Hal had obviously gone up and down the hallway of the hotel knocking on every door. All of the other guests were out of their rooms and looking at the scene in front of *our* room—Pepper and me looking at the painting of ourselves.

That's when Hal decided to make his appearance. He strode out of Mom and Dad's room, which was next to ours and at the end of the hall. He was wearing one of those berets you sometimes see painters wear and he was carrying a brush and a painter's palette (the thing with the paint on it). He bowed to all the people standing in the hall and—can you believe it?—they were applauding.

"Ah," he said, looking at Pepper and me. "I see you've found my latest creation. I'm hoping one day it too will hang in the Uffizi Gallery. What do you think?"

I tried to smile at all the people in the hall who were laughing and still applauding, you know, like I was a good sport. Pepper wasn't doing any pretending.

"Oh, there's going to be a hanging, all right," she said, "but it won't be a painting and it won't be in any gallery."

Then she slammed the door. Which would have been much more dramatic if I hadn't still been in the hallway. After a few seconds Pepper opened the door, reached an arm out into the hall and pulled me into the room. Then she slammed the door again. Yeah, not nearly as effective. Even with the door closed we could still hear pretty well everyone on our floor laughing and clapping like my brother was the best thing going.

And I could hear Hal's irritating little rat voice, too. "Thank you, thank you," he was saying. "I have some photos of myself"—I could imagine him holding them up high for all to see— "and I will be happy to autograph them for you for a mere five dollars apiece. Just step this way."

———

It hadn't gone well. Pepper and I were sitting in Inspector Rebussiani's office. I could tell he wasn't buying much of what we were saying. He was being polite, but that was about all.

"I want to thank you for bringing me this new . . . information . . . and your theory about where the kids are being held. I'll have a couple of our associates in Siena look into it."

We had just told him all about the disappearing guy in the paintings and the Caravecchio legend (he already knew about that). Then we suggested that it might be a good idea to look for the missing kids in Siena, since that's where all the pointing by the man in the red shirt and cloth cap seemed to be indicating.

Like I said, the inspector didn't exactly jump all over our theory. And I had the distinct impression that having "a couple of our associates look into it" would add up to a big fat zero.

A couple of minutes later Pepper and I were standing outside the police building in the blazing Florence sun looking at each other.

"Well, what now?" I shaded my eyes from the mid-morning glare.

"I don't know." Pepper shook her head. "I don't think he thinks much of what we told him."

"Not much doubt about that," I agreed. "Which brings us back to my earlier question . . . what now?"

"Okay, let's say that this guy Caravecchio is the real deal. I mean, we've encountered vampires and robots and we've travelled back a thousand years in time. Is this any stranger than that?"

"That's kind of what I've been trying to tell you."

Pepper nodded. "I know you have. And I know I haven't

been, like, totally listening to you. But now I am. I've been thinking about it and just because I haven't seen the guy doesn't mean he isn't out there. So if the guy in the red shirt is also the real deal—"

"Actually they're the same guy."

"What?"

"Caravecchio *is* the guy in the red shirt."

Pepper nodded again. "Oh, yeah, that's right."

"Uh-huh."

"And if he's sending you a message that the kids are being held captive in Siena, then we should be doing something about that."

"We just did," I reminded her. "We told the cops."

"And the cops didn't seem all that interested."

"True, but I don't know what we can do about that. It's not like we can just head off to Siena or something."

"Yeah, I guess," Pepper said slowly.

So you can imagine my surprise—Pepper's too—when we got back to the hotel and the first words out of Dad's mouth were, "What do you two think of going up to see the Palio. After all, that's what Hal's painting is all about and we're so close to Siena, why not go up there and catch the race?"

"I've read about Siena," Mom added. "It's supposed to be a beautiful place. And the Palio is like the running of the bulls in Pamplona, Spain or the Stampede in Calgary. It's one of those things it would be really fun to see. Don't you think?"

Pepper was nodding and grinning like crazy. Hal was standing behind my parents giving Pepper and me the thumbs-up.

I didn't know what to think. Part of me wanted to see what we could do about finding the two missing kids. But the other part of me was all *oh crap, not another Salt and Pepper mystery.* I'd promised myself that wouldn't happen this time, hadn't I?

Oh, did I say two missing kids? Make that three. Later that night we got a call at the hotel from Inspector Rebussiani. Roberto, the cute Italian guy who had also been one of the winning artists, had disappeared. He'd been gone all day.

According to the inspector, Roberto's disappearance had all the hallmarks of the other two kidnappings. Which meant that Roberto, the cute Italian guy, had also been kidnapped. I know I shouldn't have been focusing on the fact that he was cute at that exact moment. But he was ... cute. And missing.

10

Hal Disappears (Almost)

Of course, that meant *another* trip to the police station for *another* meeting.

Inspector Rebussiani's office was getting more crowded all the time. At this meeting the families of all three missing kids were present as well as the Bellamy entourage— my parents, Hal, Pepper and me.

At first I wasn't too sure just why we were at the meeting. But Inspector Rebussiani wanted to go over everything that had happened. He was looking for similarities in the way the kids had been abducted. And differences.

Of course nobody knew exactly how or where the kids were abducted, since each of the three victims had been alone (one shopping, two exploring) when they disappeared.

After he'd had the three families relate everything they could think of that might have some bearing on the case, he turned to Pepper, Hal and me.

Since Pepper and I had had the best look at Shark Teeth and her pal/assistant/boyfriend/bodyguard, he had us describe the two of them. That would have gone better if Pepper and I had been able to agree. I was pretty sure the guy was skinnier and the woman taller than what Pepper thought. And she was convinced that the guy's hair was blond. I was positive it was black but after a while I started to doubt myself. We settled for sort of reddish-brown.

It got tricky when Inspector Rebussiani brought in a police artist to try to create a picture of the two of them based on what we had seen. Of course Hal had only seen them for a brief moment but my brother "the artist" was sure he could do a better job than the police artist. So he listened in on the conversation and doodled away on a piece of paper the police artist provided. When we were finished, Pepper and I pretty well agreed on the rendering by the police artist.

Hal's creation, on the other hand, looked more like a cartoon version of Cruella De Vill from 101 *Dalmations* and Curly from the *Three Stooges*. Pepper laughed when she saw it. I tried to keep from laughing because I knew we were supposed to be serious—this was a kidnapping case, after all—but I was relieved to see that my amazing brother was still just as capable of producing crap as he'd always been.

Inspector Rebussiani did not even mention the whole Caravecchio and man in the paintings part of the mystery. Apparently he hadn't thought that was worth spending much time on.

After the meeting at the police station, we headed back to the hotel to pack and get ready for the trip. The Palio was just a couple of days off and we all wanted to get to Siena. Mom had Googled like crazy and said there was some excellent stuff happening in the days leading up to the race.

All of us went along with Dad to rent a van; then we returned to the hotel to pack up. Dad parked in front of the hotel and we climbed out and started for the entrance. As we got to the front door, a huge guy who looked like he was a wrestler or a defensive end—or both—came out of the hotel's revolving door and crashed into us, scattering us like bowling pins.

Mom lost her balance and almost fell. Dad reached to catch her while Pepper and I both got mashed up against the brick wall next to the door. That's when I heard my brother yell.

"Hey, what do you think you're doing? Lemme go!"

I looked over my shoulder just as the creepy giant guy was picking up my brother and tucking him under his arm like you'd carry a sleeping bag.

I bounced off the wall and dived at the guy, punching him as hard and as often as I could on a back that was the size of Montana. Pepper saw what was happening and didn't hesitate. She went for the low tackle and got hold of one of the guy's ankles. That gave Mom and Dad a chance to recover and they leaped into action as well, hollering as loud as they could for the cops and pulling on my brother to get him free of Mr. Creepy.

Finally the guy let go of Hal, jerked his leg away from Pepper and charged off down the street. Even as big as he was he disappeared before we could see where he went or even what he looked like, other than gigantic.

Dad hurried all of us into the lobby of the hotel. It wasn't until we were in there and gathered around the comfy leather furniture that he spoke.

"Okay, is everyone okay?" We all nodded, although Hal made a fairly big production of checking to see if he had any broken bones or blood on various parts of his body.

Dad pulled out his cellphone and got Inspector Rebussiani on the line. He explained what had happened, while my mom added her own frequent comments (she does that whenever anyone else is on the phone).

"Just a second, I'll ask," I heard dad say, then he turned to us. "Anybody get a real good look at the guy?" Pepper and I shook our heads and this time Hal didn't try to play hero.

"I wasn't in a real good position to see much," he said.

"Huge guy, blue T-shirt, major muscles—that's about all I got," I said.

Pepper nodded. "I think he was wearing a hat but I'm not sure what kind. Oh, yeah and running shoes, brown ones and dirty." She'd have picked that up from her ankle tackle.

"Scary. He looked scary," was all Mom said.

Dad relayed the information but that didn't get us out of a return trip to the police station for more questioning—this time with a police escort both ways.

I was afraid that the episode with Hal—we were all convinced he had been the target of the kidnappers— would make Mom and Dad cancel our plans for Siena. Thankfully that didn't happen, although they did put off our departure for Siena until the next morning. And we got a speech about how it was more important than ever that we stick together and how nobody was to wander off alone, yada yada yada.

Pepper and I figured that was fairly unnecessary since it was probably only Hal who was in any danger. So far the kidnappers had only been interested in the artists—that was pretty obvious. What wasn't at all obvious was why.

The inspector had told us during our most recent trip to the police station that none of the families had received ransom demands. If the kidnappers hadn't taken the kids for ransom, what could be the reason for the abductions?

That was the thought that swirled around inside my head as I lay in bed that night. When I finally dozed off, I had this, like, totally ridiculous dream about a horse race with this one huge fat horse racing around and around a revolving door while the two jockeys, who happened to be Shark Teeth and Hal, were sitting on the horse grinning and waving two gigantic bras around and around over their heads.

Yeah, that's a dream I'd like to have again.

Memo to self: You have to kill your brother.

Soon.

11

The Prisoner in the Painting

The drive to Siena was so-o-o amazing. It was all this wonderful scenery with rolling fields of green and gold and castles that had me imagining battles between armies from neighbouring areas. And everywhere there were churches that actually made me take a breath a couple of times—they were so beautiful—and little villages that made you feel like you could move right in, learn to speak Italian and grow old eating spaghetti.

As we got closer to Siena we passed through the Chianti wine region. We stopped at a few of the wineries along the way, since Mom and Dad love wine. They let Hal and me have a small glass sometimes at home but about all it does for me is pucker my entire face. Hal tries to pretend that he's all sophisticated and loves the stuff but that usually lasts for about one sip. Then he makes some excuse to leave the table.

My favourite place was this completely walled village called Monteriggioni. Serious, the whole place is inside these huge walls with fourteen towers all around the outside. Back a few hundred years ago, the town's job was to be a fortress and guard against attacks from the armies of Florence. We drove inside the walls and there were some cool shops and houses, a church and—uh-huh—more wine.

We spent a couple of hours there before piling into the van again and getting back on the road to Siena.

"Listen up, everyone," Pepper looked up from the guidebook she was reading. "It might be useful for you guys to actually know something about Siena."

"Hel-lo," Hal snorted his reply. "Can you name the person in this car who actually has a painting of a scene from Siena hanging in a famous art gallery?"

Pepper is used to Hal's stupid statements, same as I am. "Okay, hotshot, why don't you tell me the name of the main plaza."

"Sure." Hal cleared his throat. "That's easy. It's the ... uh ... Mainio Plazio."

I could hear Mom and Dad laughing from the front seat. To tell the truth, I had to chortle a little myself at that one.

"Like I said, Brainio No Existio, listen up. I'm going to give you a little Siena 101."

Hal yawned but I thought it was a pretty good idea so I wriggled into a more comfortable position to listen as Pepper recounted what she'd read.

"The most important thing about Siena is the huge

plaza called the Piazza del Campo." She turned the book to give us a look but since she only held it in our direction for about two seconds, I saw nothing. Hal didn't even bother to look.

Pepper continued the lesson. "It's pretty much in the centre of town with lots of narrow, winding and very hilly streets leading off of it in every direction. The city is built on seven hills so there's hardly a street in the place that's level." Pepper glanced down at the book to refresh her memory.

"And, uh ... oh, yeah ... the Palio, the big horse race that will happen tomorrow—the one Hal painted—" Pepper's voice sounded totally bored when she said that part— "goes around the outside of the Piazza del Campo. The horses and riders represent the different neighborhoods of Siena, except the neighbourhoods are called contradas and there's, like, this huge rivalry between them. Plus each contrada has a really cool animal symbol to represent their horse and rider."

"Like what?" Hal was trying to sound bored but I could tell he was interested in the Palio. And why not? The kid had created an award-winning painting of the race.

"Like the giraffe and the eagle and the goose and the porcupine and the panther—there's seventeen altogether. But only ten neighbourhoods get to go in the race. The others have to wait for next time."

"Cool." Hal was fired up by this time. "I'm cheering for the panther."

"I don't know." Pepper shook her head. "There's one here I think would be perfect for you—the snail."

"Ha-ha," Hal sneered and went back to working on his bored routine.

"Oh, yeah, and the riders all ride bareback." Pepper slammed the book shut to signal that the Siena 101 lesson was completed.

"Serious?" I said.

"Totally."

"Cool." I thought back to Hal's painting. I must have been so caught up with how well he'd painted the horses—and of course, with my friend, Caravecchio—that I hadn't noticed that the jockeys (if that's what they were called in the Palio) rode without saddles.

Even with all the great scenery and Pepper's commentary, I was getting antsy. I wanted to be out of the car. So I was very glad when we finally we got to Siena. About five minutes after we arrived I decided that if I ever leave Riverbend, the place I want to live is Siena.

Our bed and breakfast was situated near the top of one of the seven hills Pepper talked about. It looked down on the Piazza del Campo and the Duomo, which is this magnificent church (Europe is all about beautiful churches) off to the left of the big plaza. It took the Sienese people 250 years to build it and even then they didn't get it totally finished. In 1339 they decided to add another part, called a nave, which would have made it the biggest church in all of Europe. But just after they started it, the plague hit and killed off a lot of the population including most of the workers. So the nave was never finished. Even so, with all the statues on the front of the church and the pulpit art panels and a floor that has scenes from the Bible inlaid right into it, Siena's Duomo was the most beautiful thing I saw in all my time in Italy.

There was a second smaller plaza to the right of the Duomo. From the balcony outside our room (Europe is all about balconies), Pepper and I had a spectacular view of most of Siena.

I wanted to head off right away to hunt for the balcony in Hal's painting. I figured if I could get myself lined up opposite the house and imagine Caravecchio standing and pointing, I could maybe get some idea of what he was pointing at. But that idea got kiboshed in a hurry when Mom and Dad decided we were going to participate in all the pre-race pageantry. Decision made. No time for exploring.

The night before the Palio each contrada has a huge dinner for pretty well everyone in the neighbourhood. I was thinking, okay, a restaurant—should be good. But the dinner the night before the Palio isn't like that at all. In every contrada, fifty-foot-long tables are lined end to end. They stretch for whole blocks or fill entire squares—everywhere you look are tables and people eating. Mom told me that about 25,000 people would be eating dinner that way that night.

With the help of my parents' friends, the Blitzers, Dad somehow managed to get us into the eagle contrada's dinner.

Dinner was fine, I'm sure, but I was having a lot of trouble concentrating on my pasta. You guys all know that the last thing I want to be is a detective and the *absolute* last thing I want to be involved in is a mystery. But the whole time I should have been eating, I had this feeling—one I didn't like at all—that I was supposed to be *doing* something; that it was down to me to find the missing kids, or at least make the first step. And I was sure that the mysterious Caravecchio and the balcony he had been standing on was a big part of this.

I looked at Pepper a few times during the meal but she seemed to be busy with other thoughts. She mouthed the word "cute" at me just about every time our waiter came over (Pepper is all about cute boys). I reminded her that the guy she thought "might be the one" was a prisoner somewhere and it wasn't cool to be checking out other guys at a time like this. After that she made a greater effort to focus on her spaghetti.

After dinner we walked through the neighbourhood waving the flags we'd bought from a vendor that was set up right next to our dinner table. Our flags had the eagle symbol of our adopted contrada on them and we waved and cheered like crazy. It was one big party and I found it impossible not to enjoy myself, even with the mystery kidnappings always in the back of my mind.

Eventually our wandering took us to the plaza, where the last-minute preparations were being made for the race. Workers were spreading dirt around the perimeter of the plaza while a chain link fence was being erected on the inside. We watched the workers for a while, then Dad and Mom went into a small café for an espresso while Pepper and Hal and I hung around outside.

We were standing there, trying to figure out what to do next, when a change came over the crowd. There was a sense of anticipation, a buzzing like the sound of a thousand bees. As we tried to figure out what all the excitement was about, several horses came careening around the track right in front of us. At first, I thought it was the real thing, and was about to head into the café to get Mom and Dad. But Hal pointed out—rightly for once in his life—that there weren't enough riders. It was a trial race, a warm-up for the big event. Except it didn't look like a trial race at all. It looked to me like the riders were pretty into it, and the crowd was going completely nuts as the horses zipped by at full gallop.

After the trial race, the streets were even more crowded with people partying and others getting ready for the big day. There were people in costumes, some in decorated carts and even a few on horseback. I looked at Pepper and Hal and I could see they were having as much fun as I was.

That's when I noticed something else.

Someone else.

Through the throngs of marchers in front of me, I could just make out a grey horse, almost white. And on the horse ... was it? Yes, it was him. I was sure of it. The old man from the balconies. The man with the red shirt and the cloth cap.

Caravecchio.

And—no surprise here—he was pointing. I followed his arm and could see a row of two- and three-storey houses on the other side of the piazza. All of them had balconies and though it was a long way off, I was pretty sure one of them just might be the house and the balcony in Hal's painting.

I turned and grabbed Pepper. "There he is!" I had to yell to be heard over the noise of the crowd.

"There who is?" She yelled back at me.

"Caravecchio. He's on the grey horse. Over there."

I pointed and turned to show her.

He wasn't there. No grey horse. No man in a red shirt. No Caravecchio. Just the people in the procession. Marching and waving.

"Never mind," I said.

"What?"

Never mind," I said a lot louder.

Pepper shook her head. "You're weird."

"I know," I nodded. "Believe me, I know."

As the evening wore on, there were parties just about everywhere you went. People dancing and singing everywhere—in the streets, from the balconies, in the restaurants and bars. It was about the happiest I'd ever seen a crowd of thousands of people.

But I wasn't interested in parties. As Mom and Dad sipped on wine and settled into a conversation with some people from Phoenix, Arizona, I grabbed Pepper.

"Come on," I hissed in her ear. "I think I know where the house is."

"What house?"

"Duh! The one in Hal's painting. The guy on the grey horse—the guy you didn't see, but I did—was pointing right over there. Let's check it out."

Pepper nodded. I managed to tell Mom we were going for a walk. It wasn't easy since the noise was pretty much deafening. She gave me that serious look parents are so good at—the one that says *we've had this conversation before and if you forget what we talked about you'll be grounded until you're forty*. But all she yelled back to me was, "Be careful and stay together."

I nodded. The best part was that the Phoenix people were fussing over "the talented young artist from North America" and the talented young artist from North America was soaking it up like a sponge. That meant Pepper and I could actually do our exploring without Hal.

I grabbed Pepper again and we disappeared into the crowd before Mom changed her mind or Hal got tired of being adored and decided to join us. Moving through the throngs wasn't easy, and moving fast was impossible. Pepper and I clasped hands so we wouldn't get separated and inched our way toward the house I wanted to check out.

As we wove our way through the crowds, we had plenty of time to check out the street vendors. There were tons of them, and they were selling everything imaginable—souvenirs, Palio flags, T-shirts, even paintings. I didn't take the time to give the vendors much of a look. I wanted to see the balcony—*that* balcony—up close. It wasn't going to be easy. The crowd was like a slow-moving wave carrying us along—we just had to keep going.

When we finally got to the house we were looking for, there was enough of an opening in the crowd that I could get a good look at it. From this angle, I was even more sure it was the right one. And once again I was pretty amazed at how good my brother's painting was. The house was exactly the same.

I looked up at the balcony but no one was there. I guess I hadn't really expected Caravecchio to be just waiting around with handwritten instructions on how to find the missing artists, but it would have been nice. Pepper and I moved closer. There was one of those street vendors on the cobblestones right in front of the house.

She was an old woman and she was selling flags. Flags were a big deal at the Palio. Not only did every contrada have its own flag, but the winner of the race received the Palio itself, which was also a flag. No trophy, no gold buckle—a flag.

This time I took the time to look at the stuff in her booth. This old woman wasn't selling only flags. Like so many of the other vendors, she also had paintings for sale. I guessed they were by local artists. Most were just bad, I thought, but a few were pretty good. One caught my eye right off. It was of a man in a red shirt, wearing a cloth cap.

You guessed it—he was pointing. But this time he was standing right next to what he was pointing at—the door of a different house.

The door was blue and surrounded by flowers and it was on the main level of a house that looked pretty nice—actually very nice. It was hard to tell how big it was because we could only see part of it. But as I looked at it I got the definite feeling that the people who owned the place had some major euros.

But the best part of *this* painting was that Pepper could see it. And she could see Caravecchio.

"That's him," I told her.

"Hi," Pepper said to the painting. I guess she thought she should say something to the guy I'd been talking about all this time.

The lady selling the paintings looked at us like we were weird but she didn't say anything. I decided to try out my Italian.

Quant e per favore? I was hoping that I'd asked her how much the painting cost. I guess I had it right because she held up ten fingers.

"Ten what . . . euros . . . dollars?"

The old lady must have known some English because she answered without hesitation. "Dollars."

Pepper held up five fingers. Bargaining.

"Cinque," I said. Five.

"Sette," the old woman answered. Seven.

I nodded though I could see that Pepper wanted to bargain

a little longer. I just wanted the painting. I paid the old woman and said, *"Grazie."* Thank you.

"Prego." She smiled at us for the first time. Money will do that.

As Pepper and I stepped away from the old lady's tables with our painting in hand Pepper looked at me and grinned.

"Wow, that was pretty good. I didn't know you could speak the language. It's like you're totally Italian."

"Not exactly," I shook my head. "That was about everything I know."

I stepped into a doorway and motioned for Pepper to follow me. She did and together we studied the painting.

"He's pointing at the blue door of that house … if that's what it is," Pepper said.

"Uh-huh. Problem is, most of the painting is Caravecchio and the door. We can't even tell for sure if it *is* a house."

"If it is, it's a fancy one."

"Uh-huh."

Pepper stepped back out into the street and looked up and down. Then she looked at me and shrugged.

"I don't see a lot of blue doors on these houses, so that's good. If they all had blue doors we'd really be in trouble."

I stepped out of the doorway and tucked the painting under my arm. "We're still in trouble if you ask me. All we know is that maybe the place we're looking for has a blue door and it's sort of off in that direction." I indicated the approximate area at which the Caravecchio figure in Hal's painting had been pointing.

We both looked off in that direction.

"Whoa," Pepper said.

"Yeah," I agreed. "Houses. A lot of houses. Streets full of them. It would take us days to go up and down all those streets looking for blue doors."

"Do you have any better ideas?"

I thought back to our last escapade. Pepper, Hal and I had divided up Anchorage, Alaska and searched for a place that might have a case with a stolen book in it. It hadn't been fun—or very successful. I wasn't looking forward to doing the same thing in Siena.

"No," I admitted. "No, I don't have a better idea."

I figured we'd better get back to Mom and Dad and Hal before my parents started to worry. Again the churning crowds made it tough to make much headway but eventually we made it back to where we'd left them. Hal looked bored and unhappy.

"Great," he came striding toward us, shaking his head. "You two wander off and leave me with these senior citizens here. Thanks."

"First of all, Mom and Dad aren't exactly senior citizens. Besides, you were so busy being a big star, we didn't want to interrupt you."

"What's that?" he pointed at the painting.

I held it up for him to see.

He didn't look at it for long. "I hope you didn't pay much for it. It's no Bellamy."

"Bellamy?" Pepper stared at Hal.

"I've noticed that most of the great Italian painters were called by their last names," he told her. "Michelangelo, da Vinci, Botticelli—so I've decided that from now on I'd like to be known as Bellamy."

"Yeah, that's going to happen," I said.

"Bellamy's okay." Pepper appeared to thinking carefully. "But you might be able to do better."

"What do you mean?" Hal looked at her suspiciously.

"Well, most people don't know this, but a lot of the big-name Italian painters actually changed their names. You know, for dramatic effect. Movie stars do the same thing."

I stared at Pepper. What was she doing? I'd never heard such crap in my life.

"Really?" Hal was suddenly interested. I think the movie star thing got him.

"Absolutely," Pepper carried on. "Michelangelo—his real name was Schwartz."

"Wow, I wonder how many people know that." Hal's eyes grew bigger.

"Actually, very few," Pepper smiled her sweetest smile.

Now I knew what Pepper was doing. She was reeling in my brother. And Hal's ego was letting it happen.

"I just think there are other names that might work." Pepper seemed to be thinking hard. Being helpful. "How about from now on you're known as Flatulence? That has a nice ring to it."

Since Hal had no idea that flatulence is another word for passing gas (as in farting) he didn't get it.

"Flatulence, eh? It's not bad. But I don't know if it's as good as Bellamy."

"Oh it is, trust me." Pepper was doing her serious voice. "And you could just change your name. Just like Michelangelo did. You don't think he'd have been nearly as famous if he'd stayed with Schwartz, do you?"

I had to admit it—Pepper was good.

"Or you could keep Bellamy, if you think it's . . . good enough." Pepper shook her head to indicate that being known as Bellamy would be very sad.

"Flatulence, eh?"

"Uh-huh." Pepper was having a lot of trouble keeping a straight face. So was I.

"Maybe you're right. I mean there's no doubt that a Flatulence would be a bigger seller than that thing you've got in your hands." He pointed at the painting I'd bought from the old lady.

"Or bigger smeller, maybe," Pepper said.

"What?" Hal was starting to figure out that there was something going on. Something that he wasn't getting.

"Nothing," I said quickly. "No doubt about it . . . . Flatulence might be just the name for you."

"I'll think about it," Hal said and walked away, watching us over his shoulder.

I bobbed my head up and down to keep from laughing out loud. Which is exactly what Pepper and I did when we got back to our room. Laughed out loud until our sides hurt and we fell into bed exhausted from the day.

And if that had been the end of it I would have slept just fine that night. But I had barely fallen asleep when I had this totally weird dream that was way too real. You know the kind I mean. This was one of those ones where you're sure you're awake when you're actually sleeping and you're positive you're asleep when you're actually awake.

But the really strange part of this dream was that everything in it was blue. It was like watching a Blue Man Group concert without the men. None of it made any sense. But it definitely got my attention.

So there I was in the middle of the night, sitting up in bed looking over at Pepper, who was sitting up in bed looking at me.

"What's going on?" She said in her sleepy voice.

I shook my head. "I don't know. I was having a totally crazy dream. It was creeping me out."

"Me too."

"You were having a dream, too?" She nodded.

"What kind?" I asked.

"A blue one."

"Whoa." Now that *really* creeped me out.

She looked at me and raised one eyebrow.

I nodded. Then we both said together, "The blue door."

I threw the covers back and dropped my bare feet onto the thick carpet that covered every square centimetre of the room.

"We have to look at the painting again," I told her.

"Which painting?"

Not a bad question. Quite a few paintings had been a part of this whole thing.

"The blue-door painting," I said. "There has to be a clue there . . . something we missed."

Pepper shrugged. I could see she was having trouble with my latest theory on mysterious works of art. But she didn't argue.

I had put the painting in our closet. I got it out and set it on the table next to the TV. I turned on every light in the room. Turns out I didn't need to.

We *had* missed something. It was pretty obvious now. The blue door was actually open a crack. And someone was looking out. The person had a gag over his mouth and his eyes had that pleading-for-help look in them.

"Lars-Erik!" The name exploded out of Pepper.

She was right. It was him. And it was obvious from the gag and the desperate look that he was a prisoner in what-ever building was behind the blue door.

We stared at the painting for a long time. "Are you thinking what I'm thinking?"

Pepper looked over at me. "I don't know. What are you thinking?"

"I'm thinking there's no way we could have *not* seen Lars-Erik in that painting before."

"That's not what I was thinking," Pepper said, "but now that you mention it, that's true. For sure I wouldn't have missed it." She said the "I" like the two of them were really close, like she was Lars-Erik's mom or wife or something.

"I'm starting to think that Caravecchio is having way too much fun with this," I said. "There's stuff only I can see, there's stuff we don't see and then we see later ... it's weird."

"It also doesn't matter." Now that Pepper had seen Lars-Erik again, she was totally fixated on him. Nothing else was going to get her attention. "What matters is that Lars-Erik is behind that door."

"And the other kids, too," I reminded her.

"Oh ... uh ... yeah, the other kids, too."

"Besides, we already suspected the house or whatever that is with the blue door was where we were supposed to look. This just confirms it."

"So what now?"

"So now we sleep. Because I'm fresh out of ideas and I'm totally sleepy and I want to go to bed. Tomorrow we'll be rested and we'll be able to think a whole lot better."

Pepper nodded and yawned as if to prove my point. "If we can actually sleep without some blue dream getting in our heads."

There was no blue dream. And we both had a great sleep. Good thing, too. We were going to need it.

12

The Race and the Chase

Mom and Dad have taken us to some pretty spectacular events over the years. We've been to the Indianapolis 500, a Stanley Cup playoff game, a concert in Central Park by Garth Brooks and a double header at Yankee Stadium against the Red Sox.

None of those were as exciting and crazy as the Palio in Siena, Italy. If the day before was nuts with the dinner and the singing and dancing, this day took crazy to a whole new level.

Pepper and I had decided we'd tell Mom and Dad about the blue door and the painting. We did that over breakfast but we left out the parts about the blue dreams and Lars-Erik.

Of course, Hal called the whole blue-door theory "another example of why girls should be banned from Planet Earth," but we ignored him.

Mom and Dad surprised us by agreeing that it would be a good idea to hunt for the blue door and even offering to help. Pepper was antsy to get started right away, but we finally agreed with my parents that the search should wait until after the race. It would be almost impossible to move in most of the city until it was over anyway.

I know it's sort of our job as kids to second-guess our parents but I have to give both Mom and Dad credit—they had worked pretty hard to make the holiday great and so far, except for the whole kidnapping thing, it had been. And now Dad surprised all of us by announcing that (with the help of the Blitzers—again) he had secured us a balcony spot in a building right on the race course.

Mom wanted to know how much that had cost but Dad just smiled and said, "This isn't something we'll do every year."

Go Dad.

A couple of hours later we were in that balcony looking out at one of the most amazing sights I had ever seen. Fifty thousand people were jammed into the square. I wasn't sure how a lot of them would actually see the race—especially the ones in the middle—but that didn't stop them from cheering. Pretty much non-stop. The noise was deafening.

And around the outside of the course, every balcony in every house was crammed with people. All of them were cheering, too. And waving flags.

Dad had even remembered to get us some more flags. These ones were also from the Eagle contrada, which was fine with Pepper and me. Except the new ones Dad brought were even bigger than the ones we already had. All of us were, like, major Eagle fans now.

Except for Hal who, of course, had to be different. He'd managed to get hold of a flag from the Panther contrada and was planning to cheer for that horse.

The day started with a parade, actually a pageant. It was huge—three hours long! And it was so-o-o excellent. There were tons of people all dressed in medieval costumes (Mom explained that "medieval" was the time period about seven or eight hundred years ago—castles, the Crusades . . . interesting times). First there was this squad of guys on horseback that looked like the cavalry in a western movie, waving swords and doing this mounted charge around the track. Then came all these people carrying flags, except they didn't just carry them—they spun them and threw them in the air. They were amazing. The noise was unbelievable—partly from all the people cheering and partly from the drummers, all wearing costumes that made them look like court jesters, but not dumb or anything, just neat.

Next came long lines of carts and floats from nearby towns—and people: city officials and nobles all walking along and looking—rich. Right near the end of the parade was the coolest part of all. It was a war chariot, drawn by these two huge white bulls. In the chariot was the Palio itself, the banner that would be awarded to the winner of the race.

And finally came the riders and the horses that would

be in the race. The riders weren't on the horses; someone told us that the horses had to be blessed before they could be ridden.

While we were watching the parade, Dad told me something that I thought was strange but also kind of cool. To make sure the competition was fair, the neighbour-hoods drew for what horse their rider would have in the actual race. That explained the trial races, which gave the riders a chance to get used to all the different horses.

I couldn't imagine that happening at the Kentucky Derby or the Queen's Plate but I kept reminding myself that Europe was completely different from where we lived. Wonderful in so many ways ... but different.

I didn't have much time to ponder any deep thoughts about the ways of the world. There was too much to see and hear and smell and I didn't want to miss any of it. The horses and riders were decked out in the colours of their contrada. The Eagle horse was black and sleek and looked fast. I figured we had a good chance, although most of the horses looked pretty good. Hal's Panther horse was grey and his rider looked mean.

Mom told us that there weren't many rules in the Palio. The riders can hit the other riders with their whips or their fists but they can't hit the other horses. The rider for the Eagle contrada didn't look much older than Pepper and me and he looked really nervous. I wondered how he'd get along against the other riders in the race. Most of them looked more like the Panther guy. Nasty.

Finally, after the blessing of the horses at a nearby church, it was time. All the horses lined up on the far side of the square. We could barely see them. There wasn't a starting gate or anything, just a rope in front of nine of the horses, with the tenth horse tucked in behind all the rest (another one of the rules). Just our luck—the Eagle horse was the one in the back.

It took a long time to get the race started mostly because it was almost impossible to get all the horses in the right place and standing quietly at the same time.

Just when we had all begun to wonder if there would even be a race, the Palio began. And as loud as it had been up to that time, the noise level doubled. We did our part, too, screaming and cheering and waving our flags like the most diehard residents of Siena.

We couldn't see exactly what was happening but the crowd's cheering sort of let us know. Every time one horse moved ahead of another there'd be a huge roar. I could see that the Eagle was moving up through the crowd of horses and was about in the middle.

They were about to pass right below us! I couldn't believe how fast they were going. Every muscle in every horse was straining and every rider was totally focused on nothing but winning the race.

The best part was that our Eagle horse was moving up even faster! He pulled up alongside the Panther and I could tell he would soon be in the lead. That's when the Panther rider reached over with his whip and cracked the Eagle

126 ‡ THE PRISONERS AND THE PAINTINGS

rider hard on the shoulder. For a second I thought our guy
would be able to stay on, but when the Panther guy hit him
again, he fell off and landed hard on his side. It figured that
the guy Hal was cheering for would be a complete creep.

Another one of the strange rules of the Palio is that the
first horse across the finish line is the winner even if the rider
isn't actually on the horse. Which would have been fine
if our horse had kept running with the others. But apparently, our Eagle horse was unaware that horses like to stay
together. Because when his rider came off—he stopped!

He stopped dead. Didn't move a muscle as the rest of
the horses went careening off around the bend in the
direction of the finish line. Our horse looked over at our
rider who was on his feet and getting some attention from
what looked like medical people. The horse nickered and
looked around. But he did not run.

I looked at the horse and at the rider. It was obvious that
this year's Palio would not be going to the Eagle contrada.

And that's when I screamed. Not because of the horse
or the rider or anything to do with the Palio. Uh-uh. I
screamed at that exact moment because that's when I happened to see them right there on the street below us—not
watching the race at all, but looking up at our balcony.

Shark Teeth!

Next to her was the tall skinny guy we'd seen at the
gallery and next to him was the giant creep who'd tried to
grab Hal.

I froze for a second, my mind working furiously. It was

obvious they were watching us. Which meant they had known where we'd be. Which meant they had to have been following us.

And the fact that they were watching us meant they must still want Hal. As I stared down at them something in me just snapped. These people were dangerous. They had kidnapped some kids and they wanted to do the same thing to my brother. And I wasn't about to let that happen.

I grabbed Pepper and pointed. There was no sense trying to talk to her since she wouldn't have been able to hear me anyway. Luckily, I didn't need to.

Pepper spotted them right away. I pulled on my dad's sleeve trying to get him to look as well. But he had the binoculars up to his face and was totally caught up in the race. I looked over at Mom. She was just as focused as my dad was.

And Hal? Forget about it. Even if he'd been able to hear me, I'd have had to spend five minutes explaining and arguing. I didn't bother. Instead I took hold of Pepper's arm and pulled her back into the room, away from the balcony.

For a girl who can be pretty ditzy, there are times when Pepper figures things out fast. This was one of those times.

We charged for the door, down the stairs and out onto the street. The problem once we got there was that we could no longer see Shark Teeth and her goons. That's because there were several hundred people separating us from them. I started pushing my way through the crowd.

It wasn't working. Ninety pounds of teenage girl against several tons of excited humanity was a losing proposition. I backed up and looked at Pepper. She shrugged to let me know she didn't have a better idea.

Then to make matters worse, the crowd started pushing back. At first I didn't know why. Then, finally, I saw a rusted-out van blasting its horn and edging its way through the crowd. I couldn't believe it! What was a vehicle doing in the square during the Palio? And what was it doing forcing its way through a bunch of people who were now getting pretty mad?

I should have known! At the wheel of the van was the tall guy—Shark Teeth's partner. She was in the passenger seat next to him. I figured the giant crusher-guy was probably in the back.

"They're getting away!" I yelled at Pepper.

They must have realized we'd spotted them and decided to make their getaway. "What do we do?" (Pepper had to yell it twice before I could make out what she was saying.)

There was a sizable opening in the crowd now and there was no doubt about it—the bad guys would be gone if we didn't do something soon.

But what? We'd never be able to keep up with them on foot. I looked frantically around for something, anything, I could use to stop them or at least slow them down. But short of throwing my flag at the van I couldn't come up with any other ideas. (By the way, I did throw my flag. It did exactly zero good.)

"Come on!" I yelled as loud as I've ever yelled in my life. "Follow me."

I didn't have time to make sure that Pepper was actually following me, or even if she'd heard my banshee yell. Luckily she had. I turned and ran, not after the van but toward the horse. The horse of the Eagle contrada was just a little ways away—still standing not far from where his rider had hit the ground.

There was only one thing I could think to do. Pepper and I were going after that van—on horseback. I ran past a throng of people, some of them helping the fallen rider and some of them doing what people do when there's some kind of wreck or unexpected crisis—just standing there, watching.

Well, Pepper and I would give them something to get excited about. I climbed over the barrier fence and leaped up onto the back of the black horse. Pepper was right behind me. No surprise there. She loved this stuff. I reached down and pulled her up.

And that's when all the people who were standing around watching decided to do something more. They yelled. They yelled a lot. I'm pretty sure they were yelling at Pepper and me, and I don't think it was friendly stuff. I didn't understand any of it but even if I had it wouldn't have stopped me.

I dug my heels into the sides of the black horse and turned him in the direction of the van. Luckily, there was still a hole in the crowd that hadn't filled in after its departure. Of course, there was one small problem: there was a fence between where we were and where we wanted to go. Not a tall fence but a fence just the same.

Some horses love to run. Some love to jump. And there are some that enjoy both. I was hoping very hard that the Eagle horse was one of those. If not, Pepper and I would soon be lying on the ground on the other side of the fence, while the horse stood stock still behind it.

It would probably hurt. And we would look very stupid. That might hurt more.

But I didn't have time to think about that. Because the Eagle horse apparently had decided that all he needed was someone on his back to get him back in the mood for running.

He was running hard. And the fence was getting closer. I tried to remember my Pony Club training from years before—the part about getting my body and the horse's body ready for the jump.

At the last minute I yelled, "Okay, Eagle, jump!"

I guess maybe if I'd thought about it I wouldn't have bothered, since there was almost no chance that Eagle could actually understand English.

But he didn't hold that against us. He cleared that fence as if it was something he'd been doing all his life.

Pepper almost crushed my ribs as we went up and over, but when we hit the ground on the other side and were both still on the horse, she screamed, "Alright, baby!" as loud as she could.

Personally I thought that was even stupider than, "Okay, Eagle, jump," but I was a little too busy to tell her. The three of us burst through the opening in the crowd and went clattering down the cobblestone street in pursuit of the bad guys.

The first thing I noticed was that the streets in this neighbourhood were about the narrowest I'd seen since we got to Italy. All streets seem to be narrow in Europe, like wide enough for one car—barely—but these streets were more like sidewalks back home. Cobblestone sidewalks.

That's when I started to give some thought to my plan for what we would do if we actually caught up to Shark Teeth and friends. I realized there was a small problem. I didn't *have* a plan.

Still, I was determined not to let them get away. I knew Pepper felt the same way—just because she's Pepper.

We came to an intersection and had to make our first decision: left, right or straight ahead. I slowed Eagle down and was craning my head around in every direction when Pepper screamed, "That way!"

I looked and caught a glimpse of the van disappearing around a corner a couple of blocks up. I turned Eagle and we headed off in that direction. We couldn't go really fast because of the surface of the road. Eagle was wearing shoes and it could have been a little slippery on his feet. Still, he seemed to sense that we were in a hurry, and we got up the road in reasonably quick time.

We turned again when we got to the corner where I'd last seen the van. I pulled Eagle down to a walk and this time we approached the intersection with greater care. I'd decided it would be better if Shark Teeth and the boys didn't know how close we were.

Again we looked in every direction, but this time there was no sign of the van. I'd noticed that most of the streets were almost bare. Obviously everyone was back at the plaza watching the race.

Almost everyone. The bad guys were somewhere in this maze of houses and all we had to do was find them. Or the place with the blue door.

We rode slowly up and down several streets, both of us peering this way and that in the hope of spotting the van. Nothing.

"Looks like we lost them," I said over my shoulder.

"Yeah, but I hate to give up," Pepper answered.

"I feel the same way," I agreed. "Got any ideas?"

"Okay, we saw the van turn up that street back there. Maybe we should go back and retrace our steps."

I shrugged. I didn't think it would do much good but I didn't have a better idea. I turned Eagle around and we started back to the intersection where we'd lost the van.

That's when I heard the roar. We could still hear the noise of the crowd from the Plaza but this was a different roar. Louder. And much closer.

I looked over my shoulder just as Pepper shrieked. We'd found the van!

Actually, the van had found us. It was coming out of a narrow alley straight at us. And it was coming fast.

I dug my heels into Eagle's sides and we took off.

Cobblestone road or not, we didn't have the option of going slow. Not unless we wanted to be squished like winery grapes. (Remember what I said about the narrow streets?)

Trouble was, there was no place to go except down the middle of the street. And no matter how fast Eagle ran—and he could run pretty fast—the van was a whole lot faster.

I glanced over my shoulder. The van was gaining and it was obvious Shark Teeth and her pals weren't just out to scare us. If they kept going at the same speed they were going now and didn't veer off, they'd run us over in a few more seconds. I was pretty sure they wouldn't be veering off.

I felt Pepper banging on my shoulder. "There," she screamed. "Is that . . . him?"

I looked up at where Pepper was gesturing. And there he was. Red shirt, cloth cap, it had to be him: Caravecchio. And he was on a balcony. Again. Just like in the paintings.

But this time, I noticed something I hadn't noticed before. The "real life" Caravecchio looked . . . faded . . . like he was starting to disappear. What if he had only so much time to help us before he went back to being dead? I mean, normal dead. If this thought had occurred to Caravecchio, it didn't seem to worry him. As usual, he was pointing. Except this time he was smiling *and* pointing.

I felt like yelling, *I'm glad you're enjoying this,* but there wasn't time. And besides he *was* helping us . . . wasn't he?

Caravecchio was pointing at a wall. I stared at it and wondered what the heck the old guy was trying to say. Eagle would have to be Superhorse to jump that high! And there wasn't much chance we could somehow burst through the wall since it was made of brick.

I turned Eagle and headed for the wall anyway, mostly because I didn't know what else to do. I mean, wasn't Caravecchio supposed to *help* kids? I was hoping real hard that he was helping us now.

Sure enough, as we got close to the wall I saw an opening—just big enough for a horse and two riders to get through, and definitely not big enough for a van.

I didn't slow down. If I was wrong about the size of the opening it was going to be a little hard on our legs as we rocketed through there. But we made it, legs intact and just in time. As the van went screaming past, I pulled Eagle to a stop. We had to act quickly. I was sure Shark Teeth and Company would slam the van into reverse and be back outside the alley opening in about thirty seconds.

That's when I saw the other opening—this one at the end of a pretty garden, by a huge cypress tree in the corner of what looked like a backyard. This time there was no Caravecchio to guide us along but I knew we couldn't hesitate. To emphasize the point, the sound of squealing tires could be heard from the street on the other side of the first wall.

I guided Eagle toward the opening. As we went through we found ourselves in a series of backyards. Italian backyards are a lot smaller than the ones at home—with vegetable and flower gardens, little olive groves and sometimes even pathways and benches.

There was no one around, which made everything feel kind of weird. These were people places, but there were no people in them. Didn't *anybody* stay home when the Palio was happening?

The other weird thing was the gates—little doorways that connected all the yards with one another. And all those gates were open! It was as if someone had gone along before us preparing the way. Except that it was a maze. Which gate should I choose first? And which one after that?

"We better get a move on," Pepper reminded me. She was right. I could hear car doors closing which meant Shark Teeth and the gang would be coming after us any minute.

I guided Eagle around the gardens and picked an opening I thought looked like a good choice. We rode through first one gate then another . . . and another. We kept moving through yard after yard. Eventually I lost track of how many yards we'd passed through. Let's just say it was a bunch. Finally, I pulled Eagle to a stop, partly for a rest and partly because I figured we were pretty much totally lost.

I looked back in the direction we had come from. No sign of the bad guys. But what I did see was even weirder than having all the gates open for us. Now they were all closed!

I looked around and I am absolutely certain there was no one—not one single person—in sight. "Pepper, have you noticed—"

"Yeah, I have," she interrupted me. "But we haven't got time to think about that right now. They're probably still after us."

"Any idea which way we should go?"

"Not really."

But our decision had already been made. Before, when we'd stopped, there had been several gates to choose from, each one opening into a different yard. Now there was only one.

"I take it we're supposed to go there," I pointed.

"Looks like it."

In the next three or four yards we passed through there was always a gate—one gate only—open into the next yard. After a while, we made our way into a yard that was bigger than the rest. The house was bigger, too, and fancier, even though it looked old . . . actually ancient. It was three storeys high and had a balcony (of course) on the second storey, overlooking the yard where we were standing. I noticed that the fence around the yard and gardens was taller here, almost as if it was meant to ensure privacy.

Oh, and something else. There was no open gate in this yard. Apparently, we had come to some kind of destination. Like someone wanted us to stop here and wasn't giving us any choice in the matter.

But none of those things was the real big deal about the house. No, what was the *really* big deal about this house was the door that led out into the backyard.

It was blue!

13

The Blue Door

Pepper slid down off Eagle's back. I followed her to the ground. Neither of us said anything. It was one thing to find the house with the blue door. It was another thing to know what to do.

"We never would have found it," Pepper said softly. "Not in someone's *back* yard."

"Not without our old friend Caravecchio helping us along," I agreed.

We both stared at the door as Eagle wandered off to nibble grass.

"Got any ideas?" Pepper asked.

"Not one," I shook my head. "You?"

"Nope."

That wasn't good since it was usually Pepper who came up with ideas (not always good ones) and then it was my job to follow along. So far, thanks to Caravecchio, who for a long time seemed to want to communicate only with me, I had been leading this parade.

I didn't like being the leader. And even more, I didn't like the thought of what might be behind that door.

"I guess we have to get in there somehow."

Pepper nodded. "Oh, yeah," she said, a little too enthusiastically for me.

I looked at her. "And if we knock on that door and Shark Teeth and those two gorillas happen to be standing there, what then?"

"Good point. I wasn't actually thinking of knocking on the door," she said. "I was leaning more to—"

"Breaking in," I groaned out the end of her thought.

"Yep," she grinned.

This was the kind of stuff that really got Pepper's motor running: a mystery, missing kids, and now, best of all, the chance to sneak into a house that could be full of danger. Yeah, nothing but fun there, alright.

I looked around, hoping that Caravecchio or Inspector Rebussiani or Mom and Dad—anybody—had magically arrived to help out.

There was no one.

I shrugged. "I . . . guess so."

"Okay, let's go," she grabbed my arm.

"Hold it." I didn't budge. "We can't just go barging in there in broad daylight. We need a plan."

"Cool, let's plan."

I looked at the house and tried to get my brain into plan mode. It wasn't working.

"I really hate the idea of going through that door," I said.

"Me too," Pepper agreed.

"You do?" I was surprised.

"Yeah, I have a better idea. Up there." She pointed to the balcony.

"And how exactly do we do that? Last time I looked neither of us had wings."

Pepper turned and pointed at Eagle. "The four-legged stepladder."

It wasn't the worst plan I'd ever heard. If Eagle would stand still, we'd be able to stand on his back and climb up over the ornate cement railing and get into the house.

Breaking into places hadn't turned out all that well for us in the past—whether it was English manors or dilapidated old houses in Riverbend or thousand-year-old caves or public libraries. It tended to be dangerous and definitely scary. And I didn't think this time would be any different.

Still, if the kids were in there we had to do something. And probably sooner would be better than later. I walked over to Eagle, took hold of the rein and led him to a spot under the balcony. I wasn't sure whether he'd stand still while we did our climbing thing but he seemed pretty tired from the race. He lowered his head and went back to chewing on grass.

"Okay, Buddy," I told him. "Your job is to stand right

there. And it wouldn't hurt if you were to warn us if someone comes along."

"You keep forgetting this is an Italian horse."

I hadn't forgotten. Mostly I was talking to keep myself calm.

"Let's get moving," I told Pepper and gave her a leg up onto Eagle's sleek back. Once up there she reached down and helped me. Then we stood up gingerly, hoping Eagle didn't suddenly spook. Actually, he seemed calmer about the whole thing than I was.

"Who goes first?" I said. You might remember from one of our previous adventures that balcony climbing isn't my best thing.

"Me," Pepper said and immediately reached up and pulled herself over the railing.

That made it my turn. I tried to do it the same way Pepper had but she's much more athletic than I am. It took some grunting and Pepper grabbing the back of my shorts to get me up and over the railing.

"Well, that was easy," I said as I caught my breath and tried to look like it was no big deal.

"Good, because the getting down is going to be harder," Pepper said.

"Why's that?"

She pointed over the edge. I looked down. Eagle was in the process of wandering off in search of a better lunch. I should have thought of that.

What that meant was that we'd have to go *through* the

house to get out. Suddenly I just wanted this part of the Siena experience to be over.

I looked at the sliding glass door going into the house. It was partially open. I tried to look in but the glass was that stuff you can't see through. Pepper squinted into the open crack but shook her head. I didn't know whether that meant she couldn't see anyone or that she couldn't see period. I didn't get the chance to ask her. She pulled on the door and got it to slide further open.

We found ourselves staring into a real nice house— what looked like the living room. Pepper took one step. Then I took one. She took another one and we went like that until we were all the way into the room.

There was no one there and no noises coming from anywhere in the house. It sure seemed like we were alone. Both of us took deep breaths and looked around. There was nothing all that unusual about the place. Very expensive furniture, lots of what appeared to be very nice and very old paintings on the walls. A lot of money lived here, that much was very clear.

But nothing about it looked evil. It wasn't one of those places that made you think some boogie man would jump out of the closet at any second. And, best of all, it was still quiet.

That's the part I liked best. I don't know what I expected, the scream of a chainsaw or some buzzing sound or maybe some thumping.

Whoa. There *was* a thumping sound. Just then. Not

loud and not a lot of thumps, maybe four, but thumping for sure.

Pepper heard it, too. "Okay, so where did that come from?"

I shrugged. "I don't know."

"Somewhere downstairs, I think."

I nodded. "Yeah, that's what it sounded like."

Neither one of us made a move to actually try to investigate the sound. I looked at Pepper. Pepper looked at me. And both of us realized that looking at each other wasn't going to tell us much.

"I'll go first," I said.

I kind of hoped that Pepper would try to talk me out of that, but she didn't. I moved slowly out of the living room into a hallway that connected the room we were in to a kind of parlour or sitting room or something. Another rich-looking room. There was a spiral staircase in one corner leading down to the ground floor.

I looked over both of my shoulders (I noticed Pepper was doing the same thing), then tried to crane my neck around to look down the stairs. The trouble with a spiral staircase is that it's hard to see to the bottom.

I led the way as slowly and as quietly as I could down the stairs. Pepper wasn't far behind. The thumping had stopped, as far as I could tell. We got to the bottom of the stairs and found ourselves in a kitchen, though maybe kitchen isn't quite the right word. It was this incredible room with very modern appliances all built into rock walls that looked like they'd been there for a few hundred years.

If the pounding in my chest hadn't been reminding me how scared I was, I might have taken the time to enjoy the place. Even Pepper thought it was cool. I could tell by the way she kept turning around and shaking her head.

"Any idea where the thumping might have been coming from?"

She shook her head. "It seemed like it was from down here somewhere."

We checked out the kitchen again. A hallway led off in one direction and we started that way. We'd only taken a couple of steps when we heard it again. *Thump, thump, thump, thump.* Four thumps. Same as last time.

But where was it coming from? It seemed almost like it was coming from the stove. But that was impossible. Even so, Pepper opened the oven door and peered inside.

"This isn't Hansel and Gretel," I said. I was probably grumpier than I needed to be, but I was getting frustrated with this whole thing. Oh, yeah, and I was scared.

Pepper ignored me, which was probably a good idea, and we both stared at the stove.

"The noises aren't coming from *in* the stove," I said. "They're coming from *behind* the stove."

Pepper stared at the stove some more. "Behind the stove is a stone and brick wall," she pointed out.

"Uh-huh," I nodded. "But what's *behind* the wall?"

Pepper shrugged. "Outside?"

"Maybe . . . or maybe not. Let's go outside and take a look."

We walked over to the back door, opened it a crack and peered outside. It was as deserted as it had been before. More actually, because now there was no sign of Eagle. He must have jumped a fence or found an opening, but there was no doubt about it—he was gone. If there was going to be any kind of getaway, it would have to be on foot.

We stepped out into the backyard and made our way around to the kitchen side—the side we figured the thumping noises had been coming from. And there it was: a stone addition—a pretty big one—sticking out from the rest of the house. We looked at it and then at each other.

"I wonder if the artist kids could be—" I said.

"Me too," Pepper finished my thought.

"Can you see any way in?"

We walked around the outside of the structure. There was no door that we could see, no windows either. If there had ever been either doors or windows they were closed in with rock and brick now.

"What do you think it is?" Pepper asked.

"I'm not sure," I told her. "It might have been a stable at one time. A lot of the old mansions and castles and stuff had stables built right onto the main house."

"It looks more like a prison if you ask me."

"That's exactly what it could be," I agreed. Pepper was right. It wasn't a real friendly looking place.

"Perhaps you'd like to see inside?" For a nanosecond I

looked at Pepper to see what she'd done with her voice. But, of course, it wasn't Pepper who had just spoken.

It was a male voice and not a friendly one. Pepper and I turned around.

Behind us stood Paulo, Signore Gerusenti's assistant. On one side of him was Shark Teeth and on the other was the tall skinny guy. What was even more disturbing was that Paulo and Tall Skinny Guy were both holding guns. Pointed at us.

"That seems a bit harsh," Pepper smiled her sweetest smile. "Here we were just out for a walk and we came across this lovely home and—"

"Shut up!" Paulo barked.

"You won't get away with this," I told him. Although as I was saying it I couldn't think of one single reason why they *wouldn't* get away with whatever they were planning.

"Walk—that way." Paulo pointed his revolver toward one wall of the addition.

One thing was obvious: Paulo was the boss of whatever operation we'd found ourselves involved in. Pepper and I turned and walked. There was no point arguing.

My mind was going a thousand miles an hour. What was this all about? Kidnapped kids, an art gallery assistant who was definitely not a good guy, and a gang that was obviously up to some pretty bad stuff. But what stuff? And why?

I had a hunch we were about to find out. I also had a feeling that we wouldn't like the answers. As we got around to the far side of whatever the structure was I noticed a crack in the wall. Tall Skinny Guy stepped forward and pushed on one of the rocks. A door swung inward. We could have stared at that wall for a week and not seen the door.

Pepper and I stopped. Neither of us was anxious to go through that door, but a shove from Tall Skinny Guy kept us moving. As we walked out of the light into the dark one of the mysteries was solved. Seated at tables partway into the room were Lars-Erik, the girl, and Roberto, the Italian guy who I . . . uh . . . thought . . . was . . . uh . . . hot. (Yeah, I know, this wasn't the time yadda-yadda.)

In the painting Pepper and I had bought from the old woman, Lars-Erik had had a gag over his mouth.. There was no gag now. And he wasn't tied up. None of them were. That was the strangest part of all. All of the kids were prisoners all right. But all three of them were painting!

Captured!

As the goons pushed us further into the room, I couldn't take my eyes off what was going on. The three artists were busy working on three separate canvasses.

Of course, they stopped when we arrived and watched us being shoved into captivity. Lars-Erik even smiled a little when he saw Pepper. The other two just stared, a little surprised. I'd have to say all three of them looked pretty depressed.

"You two are no good to us," Paulo said as I turned to face our captors. "You have no talent. But you will stay here because that way we don't have to worry about you getting in the way. Salt and Pepper. And you are supposed to be such brilliant detectives." He laughed as he said that.

"Why don't you—" Pepper was about to tell Paulo exactly what he could do when he interrupted her.

"One last thing; I'll need your cellular phones."

My heart sank. I'd hoped he'd forget that little detail. I pulled my cellphone out of my purse and handed it over.

"I don't have one," Pepper lied.

"Then you won't mind if we search you just to be sure," Paulo said and nodded to Tall Skinny Guy who started toward Pepper.

I admired her for trying but I didn't blame her when at the last minute she reached into her purse and pulled out the phone. The thought of that creep getting close enough to search me made me feel ill. I imagined Pepper felt the same way.

"Now we can go get the other one." Shark Teeth grinned and pocketed the cellphone. Her grin wasn't all that appealing. "He'll be easy with these two out of the way."

"And you three," Paulo stepped around us and looked at the paintings the three artists were working on, "I need you to work faster."

Several paintings were leaning against the opposite wall and Paulo examined them as well.

"Yes, these will do nicely." He gathered them up and started for the door.

"When are you going to let us go?" the Australian girl asked. She was on the verge of tears. "You promised."

Paulo laughed and as soon as he did, Shark Teeth and the other creep joined in. "Let's go pick up Eduardo and get on with our work."

I guessed that Eduardo was the giant creep who had tried to grab Hal earlier. All three of them turned and went

DAVID A. POULSEN ‡ 149

out without saying another word. The rock door/wall was pulled back into place and they were gone.

Pepper and I both had the same thought. We dived at the door and tried to grab hold of something to pull it back open. It didn't budge. And there was nothing to get hold of. A few scratches and a couple of broken fingernails later, we gave up.

"We already tried that," Lars-Erik said. "We tried everything. It does not budge."

I turned to face him. It didn't look like any of them had been badly treated. In fact, there were some croissants and several bottles of San Pellegrino on a table behind them.

"What's going on?" I directed the question at Lars-Erik but Roberto answered.

"We are prisoners . . . hostages," he said. "They force us to paint—"

"Twenty-four seven," the Australian girl interrupted.

"Then they take our paintings and sell them," Roberto finished the thought.

"For big money apparently," Lars-Erik added. "There are people who are willing to pay vast sums for paintings by young artists in the hope that one day we will be famous and the paintings will then be worth fortunes."

"That's crazy!" Pepper said.

"Is it?" I looked at her. "Think about it. What do you think a painting by a young Michelangelo or Leonardo da Vinci would be worth? I guess there are people out there who are willing to take a chance on buying kids' paintings in the hope of turning them into big money someday."

"And not just any kids," Roberto said.

"Right. The ten most talented young artists in the world," I nodded.

Pepper nodded too. "I get it now. Pretty smart."

"What was it Signore Gerusenti told us—that Paulo had been the one to come up with the idea of a contest to find the best young artists from all over the world?"

"Pretty much, yeah."

"So that means the whole contest was cooked up to get the young artists here, take them prisoner and force them to produce paintings for these crooks."

"I think you have it figured out alright," the Australian girl said. "By the way, my name is Rachel."

"Hi," I said. "I'm Christine and this is Pepper." I smiled and Pepper nodded.

"Salt and Pepper," Lars-Erik grinned.

"Yeah," Pepper grinned back.

I just shook my head. Here we were again—up to our ears in bad guys and a mystery. And to make matters worse, now we were prisoners too. Some days I hate being the "Salt" in Salt and Pepper.

"By the way," Pepper looked away from Lars-Erik long enough to focus on me, "who do you think Shark Teeth was talking about when she said they were going after 'the other one' and that it would be easier with us out of the way?"

For the second time in minutes my heart fell into my shoes. It was obvious who she'd meant. Hal—one of the ten best young artists in the world. He might be a pain-in-the-butt little brother, but he was *my* pain-in-the-butt little brother. And there was exactly nothing I could do about the fact that he was about to be kidnapped.

"Anybody got any ideas?"

Roberto shook his head. "We have tried everything to escape. We can't get out and nobody can get in . . . unless it's the way you two did."

Nobody said anything for a long time.

Finally, Pepper tried her cheery voice. "So what now?"

Good question, I thought. Trouble was I didn't have an answer and neither did anybody else.

"One of you can take over on this part," Lars-Erik said. He held up a broom. That was obviously what had been doing the thumping. Pepper almost fell over her own feet attempting to take the broom from Lars-Erik. She took way longer than necessary getting the broom out of his hands and there was a lot of looking into each other's eyes.

I cleared my throat. Pepper tore herself away from her Danish hunk and we sat down on a couch that wasn't actually all that bad for prison furniture. The three artists went back to their paintings.

It was total silence in there.

Hours had passed; I'm not sure how many. Except for when Pepper got up and thumped the broom handle on the wooden ceiling, it was still pretty quiet in there. You'd never have guessed there were five kids in that place. There was no joking around, no teasing and almost no conversation. I couldn't imagine how tough it must have been for the other three who had been in there for several days.

I think I must have slept a bit because I sort of lost track of time for a while and developed a kink in my neck. As I was stretching out the kink, I noticed that Pepper was looking at me from the other side of the room. "I think you were right," she said. "This must have been a stable once." She was standing by what looked like a manger.

"Mm," I said. Unfortunately, knowing that this building had once housed animals wasn't much help.

I got up and walked to where the artists were working. They truly were amazing. Lars-Erik was creating a painting of a bear climbing a hill. The bear was looking back toward the artist or anyone looking at the painting. It was brilliant.

Roberto's painting was of a church in some big city. There were two little kids sitting on the sidewalk in front of the church—they looked like they might be homeless, or at least really poor. I felt a lump starting in my throat just looking at it.

Rachel's painting was a hat. Just a hat, a girl's hat that looked like it was lying on a patch of grass. I found myself wishing I could meet the girl who owned that hat.

The thing is, each of those paintings told a story—just like Hal's painting of the Palio had. I could see how people would think that art created by these kids could one day be worth a lot of money.

A noise interrupted my thinking.

"What was that?" Pepper jumped to her feet.

"I heard it, too," I said.

"It was like a crack." Lars-Erik set his brush down for the first time since Pepper and I had been thrown in there with the artists. All of us moved toward the wall where we thought the sound was coming from. Everyone was shushing everyone else like crazy so we could hear.

Crack. There it was again. Louder this time. But this time there was another sound that followed. A rumbling sound. I tried to think what would make that noise.

Another crack and then another. Finally, a small hole appeared in the wall. None of us knew what to do. Should we move toward the wall, or head away from it? Was someone coming to help, or was this just a new round of trouble? Slowly, slowly, we started forward. And stopped very fast. I heard a gasp. I thought it was from Rachel. An arm had pushed its way through the hole!

It had to be rescuers didn't it? The bad guys would have come through the door. But still, I stared at that arm without moving. An arm with a red sleeve. I couldn't see the person who was attached to that arm, but I did notice something else. The arm was pointing—indicating that we should go to the other side of the room, away from the hole. Over the last few days, I'd seen more than enough pointing, and it had always led me in the right direction. This time, I didn't argue or even think about what to do next.

I herded the others to the far corner. Roberto protested

a little but not much. And Pepper opened her mouth to argue (just because she's Pepper) but when I glared at her she shut it again and went where I directed her to go.

It took only a few seconds to find out why the arm had wanted us out of the way. There was one more crack and this time the rumbling afterward was even louder. I guess that's what it sounds like when a rock wall collapses in a heap of rubble and dust.

Some of the ceiling above the wall came crashing down too. It was a good thing we had been on the other side of the stable.

When the dust settled, there was an opening big enough for us to crawl through one at a time. As we rushed toward it, I saw an amazing sight: Caravecchio standing with his hand on Eagle's reins.

It was easy to figure out what had happened. Eagle must have kicked out behind him a few times, until his shod feet finally weakened the wall enough to cave it in. And if there was anyone in the world who knew all about rescuing kids from cave-ins it was Caravecchio.

Rachel was the first to scramble out. Lars-Erik and Pepper went through next. Roberto was set to go through but at the last second he stepped aside and gestured for me to go first. I smiled at him as I ducked my head and scrambled over the jumble of rocks to the great outdoors.

It was amazing to breathe in fresh air and see blue sky! I didn't know how long we'd been locked up in the stable but I guessed it must have been overnight. I looked around again but didn't see Caravecchio or Eagle. They'd disappeared. I was getting used to that.

We were in front of the house. The wall Caravecchio and Eagle had destroyed was the one that led to the front yard and the street.

"We better get moving." I looked around. "We know they'll be back and we better not be here when they arrive."

Too late. As I glanced up and down the street trying to decide the best way for us to go, the van came careening around the corner. It screamed to a stop in front of us, blocking any chance of escape. Paulo and Shark Teeth leaped out of the van, pointed guns in our direction. Tall Skinny Guy and the gorilla-looking character from the hotel also climbed out of the van, but not as fast. They were too busy trying to control a snarling, twisting, kicking mass of fury.

Hal!

As they set him down, Hal landed a fierce kick on the shins of Tall Skinny Guy. He was gearing up for another go when he noticed the rest of us standing on the sidewalk not far from what was left of the stable.

The expression on Paulo's face as he looked at what was left of our prison was almost funny. But not for long.

"Get in the van," he growled at us. "You may think you have done something very smart here but I assure you that we have another place for you and it won't be nearly as pleasant as this. GET IN THE VAN."

I had a real bad feeling about what might happen to all of us if we got in that vehicle. I figured it would be better if we made our stand right here on the street. Of course, there was that little matter of the guns.

I was pondering what to do about that when, once again, a rumbling sound interrupted my thoughts. I looked around to see if the rest of the stable was caving in, but that wasn't it. No. It was something entirely different, and much more strange.

A huge boulder was bouncing down the street like a bowling ball with attitude. It was coming faster and faster, gaining momentum as it travelled, and there was a fair amount of scrambling as everyone tried to get out of the way.

The boulder hit the van broadside with a tremendous crash. It was awesome. The whole side of the van was schmucked big time. It would be a long time before it went anywhere.

More rumbling and another boulder. Then another. It was like a weird pinball game. And in the middle of all the chaos, Eagle came charging down the road with two more horses alongside.

"Come on," I screamed and waved at the kids to follow me. We dashed to the far side of the street. Paulo and his gang were too busy dodging boulders to bother with us. The horses stopped hard in front of us and we mounted up—Pepper and Lars-Erik on one horse, Hal and Rachel on another and Roberto and me on Eagle.

Like the cavalry in a western movie we turned and

raced back up the street in the direction of safety. But we didn't get far.

Right ahead of us was an even greater commotion. Three police cars came squealing around the corner at top speed and barrelled toward us, right behind the latest of the boulders.

I looked back and saw Tall Skinny Guy on the ground, holding onto what looked like a broken leg. Gorilla Guy was running the other way down the street, while Paulo and Shark Teeth had climbed up on top of the van—or what was left of it. They were doing a lot of useless yelling and waving their guns around.

It was such a totally bizarre scene that I actually started laughing. I looked over at Pepper and saw that she and Lars-Erik were having the same reaction. Roberto and Rachel had joined in too. Hal was the only one who wasn't laughing. In fact, he was yelling. Stuff like, "That'll teach you to mess with me, jerks," and "Now you're going to get it," and a bunch of stuff like that. I knew that no matter what happened next, I could count on Hal to claim credit for capturing the bad guys. I'd been there before.

Speaking of the bad guys, they weren't having a real good day. The first police car screeched to a stop in front of the van. Inspector Rebussiani and two of his men leaped out, guns drawn. We were too far away to hear what was being said but Paulo and Shark Teeth threw down their guns and put their hands over their heads.

The last of the boulders took out Gorilla Guy, leaving

him in a large heap on the cobblestones. I could hear his howling even from a distance, even over all the other noise.

The third police car stopped right in front of us. Mom and Dad climbed out, followed by the other kids' parents. All of them looked totally relieved.

"Hi Mom, hi Dad," Hal called out in a cheery voice. "Nothing to worry about. I got 'em."

Didn't I tell you?

———•••———

Of course, there were countless questions to be answered and countless meetings with Inspector Rebussiani. He needed to get all of his evidence together for when the bad guys went to trial.

I found out that after Pepper and I had disappeared, the inspector had had some of his men watching Hal to make sure nothing happened. When Paulo and his gang grabbed my brother, the cops were right behind them.

The question that came up over and over was, *where had the boulders come from*. Of course, I knew the answer. But I also knew no one would believe me. No one except Pepper—maybe. Whenever anyone asked me what I thought I just shrugged like I had no clue.

But I remembered what Signore Gerusenti had told us about Caravecchio that day at the Uffizi—the part about his amazing strength as he'd moved boulder after boulder to save all those young artists. Hundreds of years later Caravecchio had done the same thing—he'd used his strength to save kids in trouble.

And there was one more thing that I didn't tell anyone else. When everything had settled down in the street that day and the bad guys were captured and all of us kids had been reunited with our parents, I happened to look across the street.

On the balcony of a house a few doors down. I saw an old man in a red shirt and an old cloth cap. It was Caravecchio. He had faded some more since the last time I'd seen him and was looking more like a spirit than before. I wasn't completely sure, but it was almost as if I could see through him. I guess that shouldn't have surprised me since the man had been dead for a few hundred years. But what did surprise me was this: Caravecchio wasn't pointing. He was smiling. At me. As I watched he turned and slowly walked into the house and out of sight.

I never saw him again.

15

My Brother the (F)artist?

"You know, you're really getting into this," Pepper grinned. "We'll make a detective out of you yet."

We were finally back home on the ranch. Pepper had come back the day before, after she and her parents had completed their family holiday. She'd said it was pretty dull compared to the earlier part of her time in Italy. No kidding! After all the excitement, I was totally enjoying the peace and quiet.

"No, I'm not and no you won't," I shook my head hard enough that I could feel my teeth clatter together. "This is the *last* time I play detective and it is absolutely the *last* Salt and Pepper Chronicle. Do . . . you . . . hear . . . me? The last. No more. Ever."

I didn't get the chance to go into any more detail about my retirement from Salt and Pepper because at that precise moment Hal burst into the room. He was . . . uh . . . upset.

"Okay, that wasn't funny, you losers," he hollered.

"What wasn't funny?" Pepper gave my brother her sweet smile—the one I thought she had reserved for Lars-Erik.

"I looked up what flatulence means." He waved a dictionary over his head.

"Good for you, Bro, increasing your vocabulary is a good thing." I grinned at him.

"*Flatulence. Having or producing gas in the intestines*," he read. "It means 'farting.'"

"You're kidding?" Pepper folded her arms. "I had *no* idea. Did you have any idea, Christine?"

"I had no idea either," I tried to look serious.

Actually, if you look up the word in your dictionary, there's a second meaning—*pompous*. It was amazing to me that one measly word could describe two parts of my brother's character so well. I didn't bother to tell him that.

"Yeah, well, just so you know, I signed my two latest paintings with that stupid name. And now people are calling me that and everything. This sucks."

I almost felt sorry for my brother. But I was too busy laughing to work up real sympathy. Pepper and I stumbled outside onto the porch to sit in the sun and enjoy some San Pellegrino to remind us of Italy.

And laugh at my brother.

And maybe talk about guys.

Don't miss
Shivers and Shakes,
Book 6 in the Salt & Pepper Chronicles,
coming in Spring 2009
Turn the page for a sneak peek!

1

Mary King's Close

Mary King's Close.

I was wishing I hadn't let them talk me into going there. To an underground street that existed as part of the city a few centuries ago. Before the plague came and killed thousands in the city including most of the people who lived in Mary King's Close. The modern city of Edinburgh has been built over the street but now there are tours that take you down to where you can see the buildings and alleys and corners and corridors, long empty, long abandoned . . . all very eerie.

They're called Ghost Tours because, as you'd expect, there are all kinds of ghost stories in a place like Mary King's Close.

"The Most Haunted Place in Edinburgh," the brochure said. It turned out that the brochure was right.

All kinds of ghost stories.

I hadn't wanted to go. I would have preferred a nice walk to the statue for Greyfriars Bobby, the little dog that stayed by his master's grave for fourteen years, guarding it and leaving only to eat. That kind of tourist spot was more my style. But my parents and Pepper's, they're all about spooky stuff—spookier than a faithful little Skye terrier. Pepper and Hal are even worse. So I was outvoted and that Tuesday evening we were under the city, walking through Mary King's Close, walking through streets that had been crowded with people a few hundred years ago.

On this night, though, there were only twelve people in Mary King's Close. I was one of them. We'd been in several shops and houses and nooks and crannies of the little underground streets as our guide, Andrew MacIsaac, did his best to talk in what he apparently thought was this totally spooky voice. To me, he mostly sounded like he had a cold.

We were near the end of the tour and I was looking forward to seeing the sky again, even if it had been getting dark when we started out on our tour. One last building—it had once been a shop, a combination dress shop and wooden furniture store. I guessed it was run by a couple, with the man selling the things he built and the woman of the house making and mending dresses and other clothing.

There was a counter where people had conducted their business and a chair in one corner and even a bolt of cloth leaning against the back wall. The paint on the walls was faded and chipped, but it seemed as if they had once been light brown. There was a doorway leading to another room, but our guide didn't take us back there.

I could almost imagine people coming and going from the shop, chatting, laughing, holding dresses up to see if they fit. Andrew MacIsaac interrupted my pleasant thoughts. He told us that the man had died horribly, the victim of a murder in 1645. A couple of years later, the woman, a widow now, had run away to escape the plague. She was so terrified that she left her own father and daughter behind when she fled.

Andrew went on to say that the grandfather and daughter, a girl of ten years old, kept up the shop for a while, until they both got sick. The little girl took care of her grandfather until he passed away, but there was no one to take care of her. She died alone one wintery night "in that very room." Andrew pointed to the doorway at the back. Clearly he liked the idea of throwing something a little scary out there for us to think about. And he really liked saying . . . "*in this very room,*" or "*in that very room.*" He said it a lot.

The thing is, I didn't think about it, the scary stuff. Not at first. Not until I heard . . . sounds. At first I wasn't sure what they were. And then I figured they were part of the tour, kind of a little play that was being put on to amuse and maybe scare us a little. Like Andrew MacIsaac's voice. As I moved closer to the doorway for a better listen, I decided that a wannabe-actress like Pepper should get in on the action, too. I turned around to tell her, but she was gone.

In fact, everyone was gone. They must have been eager

for a cup of the tea or something (being served from an ancient-looking cart in the street just outside the shop), because they'd left me all alone. I was the only one still in the shop, and definitely the only one standing in front of the doorway to the second room. I decided to take a quick peek before catching up with the group. I opened the door a crack.

It was dark and empty in there, except . . .

I listened hard. There were sounds . . . soft sounds that felt somehow like they were all around me. And only me. *In this very room.*

But I wasn't alone. The sounds were whispers—two voices, speaking to one another . . . or to me. Or maybe both, I wasn't sure.

Whispers . . .

       Whispers . . .

              Whispers . . .

"Child, please, bring me the bowl, the water . . . the water."

"Here, Grandpapa . . . drink, it will cool you and help the thirst. Then you can sleep."

"There will be much time to sleep, Ann-Laurie. Forever is the time for sleep."

I heard them talking. And as I listened I wished I had never heard of Mary King's Close. I couldn't seem to make my legs go . . . to get out of there. Instead, I kept listening to the voices. And then I saw them. I saw them because they were speaking to me.

Whispers...

Whispers...

Whispers...

"You can't help us but you must help Stephen Beecombe."

It was the little girl who was speaking. The old man was lying on a rickety old bed—a bed that hadn't been there a moment before. The little girl placed a wooden bowl in his hand and he drank slowly, his bony hands shaking. Afterwards, he spoke in a voice that was old and tired ... and dying. Or already dead. From the plague. He looked horribly ill.

Both the old man and the girl had this glow radiating from the top part of their bodies. From the chest down their bodies got fainter and fainter, until you couldn't really see their feet. It gave them the appearance of floating, although the little girl was the only one who was moving.

"You must help Stephen Beecombe." The old man spoke so softly I could barely hear him. He looked at me through watery, hollow eyes. *"And watch out for the man with the wooden teeth. Watch out for him, watch out ..."*

Then they were gone. I couldn't see them or hear them. The old man and the little girl had disappeared. Gone back to ... wherever ghosts go when they're not ... in this world.

When I caught up with the rest of my group, I didn't say anything. Not at first.

Pepper Mackenzie wants to be an actress.

That's the first thing you need to know. You also need to know that she was in this production of *Charley's Aunt* at our school (I did make-up for the show), and the production was selected to be part of the Edinburgh Children's Festival in Scotland. Which meant that the whole cast and crew headed off to Scotland to perform the play there.

All very cool, right? Well, it might have been cool if the families hadn't been invited to go along too, or if my family hadn't actually *wanted* to go along. Or if one member of my family wasn't my little brother Hal, who is sick, twisted and couldn't be left at home.

I didn't get that part. Our dog, Buck, would be staying in a kennel while we were gone. Surely there are kennels for little brothers. Or jails. Or dungeons . . . something. Why hasn't someone thought this through?

So that meant that Pepper and her family (they're pretty normal) and I (Christine Louise Bellamy) and my family (they're pretty normal—except for Hal) were all going to Edinburgh, Scotland—very old, very beautiful, and it turns out, very spooky if you happen to find yourself in the wrong place at the wrong time.

And Salt and Pepper are kind of famous for just that. Although I'm sure if you ask Pepper or Hal they'll tell you that we're all about being in the *right* place at the *right* time.

That's the difference between us. Pepper and Hal love adventure and mysteries and scary stuff (well, not too scary). I, on the other hand, like sane, sensible stuff—good books, slow summer days, chocolate chip cookie dough ice cream ... and water. All kinds of water—hot baths, swimming pools, streams running through thick green forests and the ocean.

That's one of the things I was looking forward to about Scotland. Not that I was planning to do a lot of swimming in the North Sea, which is what sits right next to Edinburgh. North as in cold water, especially in spring. But I like walking next to the ocean, looking out at the immense expanse of water and imagining being in a ship out there somewhere, or just throwing rocks and sticks into the waves. It's all good.

So you've got the ocean, Edinburgh, the Children's Festival and a school trip. Excellent. What could go wrong? Well, for starters I already mentioned my brother. Then there was the fact that everywhere we go—England, Alaska, New Mexico, Italy—there's always one more Salt and Pepper Chronicle that turns up—a mystery with bad guys and weird people (as in crooks, zombies, evil Dark Side priests from a thousand years ago, a dead guy who sends messages ... *to me*). Yeah, just the average folks anyone would want to spend time with. Oh yeah, and I didn't even mention the vampires.

You can see why I was a bite (uh, I meant a bit) nervous as we got ready to go to another foreign country where stuff just might happen ... like it had every other time.

To tell the truth, I had forgotten all about that stuff as soon as we got to Edinburgh. I loved the city instantly. We stayed in a bed and breakfast—a house that dated back three or four centuries. I liked that. Early on our first morning in the city we went for a walk on the Royal Mile, which is this amazing street that runs from Edinburgh Castle to the Palace of Holyroodhouse. I liked that. And, at least at first, instead of the grey, rainy, cold weather Edinburgh is famous for, it was warm and sunny and . . . green. I really liked that.

I especially liked the theatre where we would be performing. It was called the *Lyceum*. It was huge and ornate and was one of the most important theatres in the city. Pretty good for a bunch of small-town kids from Riverbend School.

Our week's stay in Edinburgh had started just the way I wanted it to—lots of cool Scottish people and places, a chance to experience the food and culture of an amazing country, and for the first day and a half, a miracle—Hal hadn't done anything *really* stupid.

It looked like, for the first time ever, we would actually go someplace and not be thrown into the middle of a mystery or scary adventure. Salt and Pepper, retired at last!

But there was one small problem. The Edinburgh Children's Festival wasn't the only festival going on while we were there. The other festival, which was happening at exactly the same time, was the Edinburgh Ghost Festival.

Which is how we came to be on a ghost tour of Mary King's Close one Tuesday night.

And because of that tour, our stay in Edinburgh was going to be different from the one I had planned and hoped for. Very different.